Stormy Sky N

by

Sara Bourgeois

Chapter One

It was a dark and stormy night...

Okay, it was raining, and it was dark, but the stormy thing was a bit of an exaggeration. It had been raining for days in Coventry, and people were blaming the return of the unseasonably warm temperatures.

I was personally disappointed because if not for the increased temperatures, it would have been snow. We'd had a little bit of snow around Christmas, but it had warmed up again a couple of days later.

No one really expected spring to start in January, but that seemed to be what was happening. I figured there was plenty of time for it to get bitterly cold again by February, but I also thought that perhaps we'd just been blessed with a mild winter.

Either way, I had dinner in the oven, and Thorn was due back from work at any moment. Meri was curled up around his food bowl "patiently" waiting for his dinner.

Thorn finally came through the front door, and Meri jumped to attention. He seemed to think that Thorn coming home was the signal that it was time for his dinner, and I'd just gone with it.

I filled his bowl with flaked tuna and crumbled bacon on top. All the while, I could hear Thorn taking off his boots in the entryway.

"There are dry clothes for you folded on top of the dryer," I called out when I heard him set down his second boot. "It's sweats, socks, and your unmentionables."

"Thank you so much," he said. "I don't think you understand how much that means to me right now."

I wouldn't have any idea what he meant until later when I went into the laundry room to wash his uniform. It was soaked through like he'd fallen in a lake, but I found out it was just from having to stand out in the rain. Well, actually help a nearby farmer get his cattle away from a swelling creek.

But, a couple of minutes after I told him about the dry clothes, Thorn appeared in the kitchen. He looked exhausted, and more than that, his mouth was set in a grim line.

"That smells delicious," he said and managed a soft smile.

"Tater tot casserole," I responded. "I hope you don't mind. It's a pretty simple recipe, but it's good. Should warm you right up too. You look cold. Are we finally getting some real winter?"

"I thought you were all in tune with nature and stuff," he teased.

"Lately, the only way for me to be in tune with nature is to tune into the Weather Channel. I haven't done that since yesterday, so I didn't know if we were expecting a temperature drop tonight," I responded.

"I'm sorry," Thorn said sheepishly. "I shouldn't tease you about that stuff."

"It's okay. You don't have to walk on eggshells about it," I said, but it had stung a little. Totally not his fault, though. My mood about our magical reset changed based on the day. Sometimes I was happy about it, and some days, like that day, I missed the little things like being so in tune with nature. "So, did we get a big drop in temperatures?"

"Not huge," Thorn said. "It's upper forties and lower fifties. Probably won't freeze up overnight, but that rain just had me chilled to the bones."

"Well, sit down. I'll get you a beer and fix you a plate," I said.

"I can get my own," Thorn protested.

"Just sit down and let me fuss over you a little," I said and pointed toward his usual chair at the kitchen table with the spatula in my hand.

"All right," he relented with a chuckle.

"So, are we looking at significant flooding?" I asked as I got a beer out of the refrigerator.

"We might be, but since Coventry is on a slight elevation, I'm more worried about the surrounding area. We've got some cattle and horse farms that could be in trouble with their animals, and there are a few places that will be cut off."

"Are people stocked up in case they have to hunker down for a few days?" I asked.

"That's what I've been spending most of my time doing. The county doesn't have the manpower to go to every farm in time, so my deputies and I have been going door to door making sure the people know. We've been telling people to get to town and stock up on what they need while they can and to bring their livestock back in close. I had to help one farmer get part of his herd out of danger. That's how I got soaked."

"Oh, my," I said.

"But for the most part, these old farmers are ready. They don't need anyone to tell them to be prepared for a rainy day," he said.

"Well, it's good that you're checking on them anyway," I said.

After dinner, Thorn did the dishes and I dried. We tried to watch a movie on the big screen television I'd installed over the fireplace just for him, but he fell asleep fifteen minutes in. Knowing that he was going to get up early and go running with Tangerine, I nudged him awake and told him to get his butt to bed.

While he was trudging up the stairs, I took Tangerine out back and we found the driest spot in the yard for her to do her business. The back yard wasn't totally submerged, but there were a few huge puddles forming. I made a mental note to ask Thorn if he could build one of those little doggie shelters outside the back door. I wanted one with a roof to keep the rain and snow out and I'd seen ones with a gravel floor for drainage. I'd have to think about that part, but it probably would have helped.

Lightning flashed overhead and thunder rolled over us like a thousand stampeding horses. Tangerine let out a little yelp and made a beeline for the door.

"I agree," I said and followed her back inside.

The next morning, Thorn was gone by the time I got up. I found Tangerine snoozing in the kitchen on a bed of towels. Apparently, they went running rain or shine.

I snapped my fingers to dry her off. I could still do that.

Or so I thought…

She instantly turned into a ball of floof. "Oh, my," I said. "I might have to take you to a groomer."

"Good going, lady," Meri snarked as he sashayed into the kitchen for breakfast.

"Good morning to you too," I retorted. "You're in fine form this morning."'

"You're one to talk," he sassed.

"Hey, I'm in charge of breakfast. You might want to be nice to me," I said.

"Whatever," was the response I got.

I turned my back so he wouldn't see me smiling at his rude butt. He had to wait for his breakfast because I was frying up bacon and scrambled eggs for both of us. I made an egg for Tangerine too, but she couldn't have any bacon. Once I plopped the egg down in her food dish, she didn't seem to mind.

"Are we still going to stop and see Viv?" Meri asked as he finished his breakfast. He was already trying to angle for more bacon, but I'd come to expect it.

"If we have time," I said noncommittally.

"Well, then you had better get going," Meri said.

Just then, another huge flash of lightning lit up the sky and the light from it came flooding into the house. The simultaneous crack of thunder was enough to shake the house. Tangerine ran to my feet and whimpered. Surprisingly, she had to fight for real estate with Meri. Even he had gotten spooked.

"I guess I won't be leaving you home today." I bent to scratch Tangerine's fluffy head. "You're coming with us," I concluded as I picked them both up and carried them with me to the bedroom.

The house would take care of Tangerine while I was at work, but she seemed too scared to be left alone. Normally, I would have just asked Meri to stay behind and keep her company, but Meri didn't let me go anywhere without him. He was still in hyper-protective mode until the baby was born.

"I've gotta take a shower," I said as I set them both down on the bed. "Meri, please keep Tangerine company."

"Do I have to?" he asked, but as Tangerine settled down on the bed, Meri curled up next to her.

"I think you'll figure it out," I said and left them to shower.

The good news was that I got most of the way through my shower before there was another loud crack of thunder and blinding flash of lightning. The bad news was that when the power went out, I still had shampoo in my hair. I hurried and rinsed it out before the water went cold.

"Come on, house. Really? Everything you can do, and the power is out?" As if it heard me, there was a brief flicker of the lights coming back on, but ultimately it sputtered out. "Thanks for trying," I said as I stepped out of the shower.

Fortunately, there was enough light coming through the bathroom window to keep me from stumbling around in total darkness. When I opened the door to go back out into my bedroom and get dressed, I found Meri and Tangerine waiting. They must have practically had their noses pressed against the door.

"Come on, Meri," I said as I stepped over them. "You obliterate demons with your powers, and you're totally spooked by a storm?" On cue, the house shook as thunder rumbled through the sky above us. "Man, this storm must not be moving. That sounded just as close as before. I wonder if it's stalled out over us."

"Whatever it is, I hate it," Meri groused.

"Well, let me get dressed really quick, and we'll go see if the Brew Station and my shop have power," I said. "I doubt there will be much business today, but I'd rather not hang out here without power all day."

I dressed in jeans and a long-sleeved t-shirt. It was too warm for a sweater, but I was worried that if I wore short sleeves, the power would be off everywhere. I didn't want to end up chilled to the bone.

After I put Tangerine's harness on, I loaded Meri up in my bag and put on my boots. The black Doc Martins were my favorite part of the cold season. I may not have loved cold weather or tons of rain, but I did love my boots.

I practically sprinted to the car with Meri in the bag and Tangerine tucked under the other arm. While I did manage to splash through a couple of shallow puddles, I kept my furry friends dry. I didn't bother going around to the passenger side but instead opened the driver's door and leaned way in to deposit Tangerine and Meri in the passenger seat.

Thunder crashed overhead and made me jump as I tried to get behind the wheel. I used the app on my phone to start the car and turn on the seat warmers.

It started to pour twice as hard as I backed out of the driveway. The car's sensors kicked the wipers up to full speed, and I worried that it wouldn't be enough.

"We'll make it as far as we can, but I might have to pull over," I warned my companions as I began driving down the street.

"Use the autopilot," Meri said. "I don't know why you spent thousands of dollars on that if you're not going to use it."

"I don't know," I said. "I feel more comfortable being in control, but maybe. I guess it's better than sitting in the car on the side of the road."

Fortunately, in my opinion, it never came to that. The heavy showers persisted, but the wipers were able to keep up enough for me to navigate the practically abandoned streets.

The space in front of the Brew Station was even open when I arrived, and that never happened. "Wait in the car," I said to Meri. "No sense in you getting soaked. I'll be right back."

"Fine," he said. "Just make sure she doesn't forget my bacon."

"Has she ever?" I asked but jumped out of the car and closed the door before he could answer.

It was a great day for there to not be a line out the door at Viv's place, but everyone inside looked dreary and sad. They were used to a hopping morning full of hard work and happy customers. It had to be a total drag just standing around hoping the rain would stop.

Both girls behind the counter tried to step up when I came in the door, but Viv appeared from the back at the sound of the bell over the door announcing my arrival. "She's mine, girls," Viv told them. "Why don't you guys go clean out the walk-in?"

They both groaned but still darted into the back. Nobody ever wanted to clean out the walk-in, but they were bored beyond belief. I looked around, and there was one elderly gentleman sipping coffee and reading the news on a laptop. He was probably dug in until the rain let up. Or until the Brew Station closed.

"Breakfast is on the house," Viv said. "I've got a bunch of stuff prepped, and it doesn't look like I'm going to sell it. You should take something for Reggie too. You think she'll make it into work?"

"Yeah," I said. "Jeremy bought her that new truck. I think that thing can drive through four or five feet of standing water."

"Well, I might need her to come over here and rescue me if this keeps up," Viv said. "You want your usual latte?"

"Yeah, and a raspberry mochaccino thing for Reggie," I said. "Thanks. So, Thorn said that Coventry shouldn't flood because of some sort of elevation. We're on an rise here. But the surrounding area might get washed out. The creeks are swelling."

"Well, that's good for us, then," Viv said.

I stood at the counter and watched the rain out the window while she made the coffees. She brought them over to me and then bagged up four croissant sandwiches with bacon, egg, and gruyere.

"I don't have the fryer on in the back, so I hope four sandwiches is okay," she said and slid it all across the counter to me. She normally used paper bags, but that day she doubled-bagged the entire affair in a plastic grocery bag.

"Thanks again," I said. "Four free sandwiches is more than generous."

"There's twice the bacon in there for Meri, and I saw your little puppy through the window, so there's some turkey lunch meat in there for her too," she said.

"You're the best," I said. "I'll probably come back over here for lunch. I doubt we're going to get any business today either."

"Turkey club sandwiches and all the chicken and wild rice soup you can handle. I got it started this morning in a moment of misplaced optimism. If you show up here again, expect to go home with at least one container of it," she said with a chuckle. "I don't think the girls working with me today will be able to eat it all, and they might call your husband on me if I try to make them."

"Oh, that sounds delicious. We'll definitely be back for lunch," I said.

After that, we said a quick goodbye, and Viv went into the back to help the girls clean the cooler. I ran out to my car and dove in like I was made of sugar.

Meri and Tangerine sniffed the bag, and I wasn't sure which one of them was more excited. "Pipe down, you two," I said. "We'll eat as soon as we get into the shop."

I backed out of my space, shifted into drive, and did my best to baby the accelerator. That car went from zero to sixty in under four seconds, so you had to be careful. But, I wasn't careful enough.

You would have thought I'd stomped on the pedal the way the car lurched forward and then fishtailed. "Whoa, lady!" Meri cried out as he dug his claws into the seat.

Tangerine fell over and rolled into him, but since Meri was anchored in place, they both managed to stay on the seat. I righted the car and drove as slowly as I could over to the other side of the square and parked next to Reggie's truck.

I got out of the car, and Reggie must have seen me coming because she opened the door and held it. "Run for it," she called out through the deluge.

For whatever reason, Meri and Tangerine decided to heed her call. They bounded past me and out the driver's door. Somehow, neither one of them managed to land in the puddle outside the door.

I reached back in the car and grabbed the food, coffee, and my bag. As I stood up, it became abundantly clear that I didn't have my purse straps all the way over my arm, and it did fall right into the very puddle Meri and Tangerine avoided.

"Oh, no," I said and snatched it up hard enough that I splashed water all over my thighs. "Great," I murmured as I ran for the door with my soaked bag.

Once I got inside, I dumped my bag's content out on the counter. Reggie ran in the back and grabbed a bunch of paper towels. We tried to dry everything as best we could. My phone was in one of the side pockets, so it avoided getting ruined.

I had a bunch of paperwork, including my new marriage license, in a folder that was completely waterlogged. "Crud, I needed that to change a bunch of stuff to my married name," I said.

"You could just not change it," Reggie offered with a shrug. "Although, if you go with Wilson, you won't have to spell it out for everyone anymore."

"Nobody knows how to spell Skeenbauer," I said. "Of course, they can't spell Kinsley either, but I'll never change that."

"You could," Reggie said. "You could change it to something easy like Kim."

"I don't think so," I said. "I like Kinsley, but I am going to take Thorn's last name."

"How traditional of you," Reggie teased.

"So?"

"It's fine. Just having fun with you. So what are you going to do? I don't think anyone's going to accept that marriage license," Reggie said.

She was right. It was completely soaked, the seal was flattened, and some of the ink was running. "I'm going to have to go over to the courthouse and grab another copy."

"In this rain?" Reggie asked. "Even if you run, you'll be completely soaked."

"Well, maybe I can try a touch of magic. All I'm trying to do it dry a piece of paper. Surely, I can handle that," I said and pressed it flat.

Spoiler alert: I could not handle that.

I waved my hand over the license and tried to use just a hint of fire and wind magic to dry it. It burst into flames and a second later, nothing was left but a small trace of ashes. Wet ashes because somehow the counter was still wet from water seeping out of the paper.

"That didn't go well," Reggie said.

"I would have been better off with a hair dryer," I admitted. "I hope that at some point, I can get some magic back under control."

"I thought you liked not having it. It's what you always wanted," Reggie said.

"Yeah, well, I didn't realize that there were some parts of it that I really liked having. I miss those parts," I said.

"At least the decrease in your magic doesn't seem to be retroactive. Can you imagine if we had to look our age?" Reggie lamented.

I'd nearly forgotten that my family had blessed her and Viv with youthful looks and a long life. That would have sucked if those benefits went away. Not that either of us were that old, but it sure was nice looking ten years younger and knowing you would stay that way for decades.

"On that note, I'm going to brave the rain, But I'm taking this plastic bag with me to keep the new marriage certificate in," I said as I unpacked the breakfast bag. "Will you eat and give the animals their treats?"

"I'm going with you," Meri declared.

"Really?" I looked at him skeptically. "What do you want to do, ride in the bag?"

"Fine, I'll stay here," Meri relented. "I hope you don't get into any trouble and need me."

"I'm just going to the courthouse to get a marriage certificate. How much trouble could there be?"

When I left my shop, I ran across the street and then through the square. The Christmas décor was gone, and there were no tourists milling about, so once I turned at the statue, it was straight shot to the front steps of the courthouse.

It was a good thing I wore those boots because my feet pounded against the pavement, and I splashed through several shallow puddles. The bottoms of my pants got a little wet, but my feet stayed dry.

I couldn't say the same thing for my hair. The pitying looks people gave me once I was inside the courthouse were enough to tell me I must have looked like a drowned rat. For a moment, I considered dipping into the bathroom and trying to use a bit of magic to dry my hair, but considering what had happened to Tangerine... and then my marriage certificate, I decided against it.

Oh, gawd. Poor Tangerine. She and I, more so she, were lucky that all I done was make her a floofball. I couldn't have lived with myself if I'd incinerated her, and I didn't have the powers to bring her back from the dead again.

The regular records office was on the first floor in the east side of the building. That's where you could get any current vital records. I wouldn't need to go down to the basement archives where my father had worked.

Inside the county clerk's office was a long counter that stretched the length of the narrow room. It looked as though it was built for multiple employees to handle several customers at once, but I never saw more than one person in there.

There were several desks along the outside wall set up to look out the windows, but there was no one at them. There was only one employee in the clerk's office, and I startled her when I walked through the door.

"Oh, my, you gave me a start," she said and pressed her hand to her chest.

She was a short, full-figured gal with curly hair dressed in black slacks and a stylish blouse covered in a cherry pattern. Somehow, on her, it was not the least bit gaudy. It suited her.

"I'm sorry," I said.

"Are you… real?" she asked and then chuckled nervously. "Of course you are," she said and chuckled again. "I meant to ask if you're alive, but I know you're that too. Ignore me, I'm being silly."

"Are you okay?" I asked.

"Yes," she said and got up from her desk. She walked over to the counter. "It's just that… sometimes I think this place might be haunted. People tell me I'm being silly, but on days like this when it's dark and dreary, and there's almost no one around, I could swear."

"That's interesting," I said because I could neither confirm nor deny her suspicions. I knew the place was haunted, but anything I said about it might be crossing the line. "I don't think I'd worry about it." That was a lie too. There was that one particular ghost, although I didn't think it would bother this woman down on the first floor. I'd never even heard anyone talk about that ghost before. It was as if it were just me and my mother who saw it. "I think the idea is kinda cool, but don't be scared. I guess that's kind of hard on a spooky day like today."

On cue, thunder crashed again. "I guess the storm's kicking up again," she said. "It's like it's coming in waves. Anyway, what can I do for you?"

"I just got married, and I dropped my copy of my marriage certificate in a puddle this morning. I need a new copy because I'm not done changing things to my new name," I said.

"Sure thing, I can do that," she said cheerfully. At least the task at hand had distracted her from her fears. She took my name and other information and typed it into a computer on the counter next to where she stood. "Okay, all done. It's twenty-five dollars, and you can pay with a check, credit, or debit card."

"I've got my debit card," I said and pulled out my wallet.

She ran the card and handed it back to me. "Okay, all you do is go up to the top floor and pick it up in the central processing room. It's to the right when you get off the elevator."

"What?" I asked. "I have to go upstairs to get it?"

"Yeah, we've had a lot fewer requests over the years for physical copies of documents, and the county decided that we didn't all need printers anymore. The whole building prints up there now. There are only two actual printers. There's a lady named Tammy behind the desk, and she'll give you your document when you get up there," she said.

"Okay, thanks," I said as I tried not to reveal how much I did not want to go up to the top floor.

I made my way from the county clerk's office over to the elevators and forced myself to push the button. A creeping feeling of dread was already snaking its way up my spine when the doors opened.

"At least it's empty," I said to no one around me and stepped in.

As soon as the doors closed and I hit the button for the top floor, it felt like there was someone in the elevator behind me. Every time I looked back over my shoulder, there was no one there. No one that I could see, but I could feel something. Whatever it was, it was cold. So much so that it almost felt like there was icy breath on the back of my neck, but it was a full feeling. It was more like the whisper or idea of a feeling.

"That means it's in your head," I said to the empty elevator.

It was the first time in a long time that I'd been without Meri, and I nearly wept with relief when the elevator doors opened and I could exit the tiny, suffocating space.

I turned to my right and started down the hall to find the central processing office. When I got to the end of the hallway, I realized my mistake. I was a grown woman, and witch, who often mixed up my right and my left. I should have had an L and an R tattooed on my hands, but then everyone would know my shame.

So much for getting the document and getting out of there quickly. Despite walking nearly the entire length of one side of the building, I hadn't run into anyone else. Either not many people worked on the top floor, they were all off that day, or they were quietly working in their offices in tandem.

It struck me as I walked past one particular window that... it was the one I always saw the ghost with the black eyes and black gaping maw of a mouth staring down from when I was in the square. I was standing there in her spot, and suddenly, I felt compelled to stop and look down. I wanted to see what she saw.

I watched the rain for a minute. It was a beautiful view of the square, and it must have been magnificent when the sun shone. You could watch all of the people coming and going from the shops and the Coventry Library on the opposite side of the plaza.

The loneliness of someone or something trapped there just watching and never able to join must have been overwhelming. I could feel it down into my bones.

And then I could feel icy fingers wrapped around my throat. Instinctively, my hands flew up, and I tried to pry them away. But, while they were cutting off my windpipe, the hands weren't really there. I could not breathe, but I couldn't fight it either.

I needed Meri, but he hadn't come with me. Why had I discouraged him from coming with me? I knew this specter resided in the courthouse. I never thought I'd have to come up to the top floor, and I'd only ever seen her leave her spot once. That was for very specific purposes. Or, so I'd thought.

As I closed my eyes and prayed to the Goddess to save me, I also promised to stop acting like I knew everything. "If you let me live, I'll be a more humble student," I whispered through the hands clutched around my throat.

The ghost didn't let go, but she lost her grip enough that I could turn and run. I pulled away from her, and I could swear I heard her banshee screeching behind me, but at the same time, it was all in my head.

When I passed a stairwell, I didn't even bother with the elevator. There was no way I was going to push a button and wait for that thing to arrive.

I threw open the door to the stairs and ran down them as fast as I could without falling on my face. "Feet, don't fail me now," I said as I bolted down several flights of stairs.

There were a couple of people in the courthouse lobby when I burst through that door. They looked at me like I was crazy when I ran through the lobby and out into the rain. I didn't care. I was out of there.

When I got back to the shop, dripping wet, pale, and without the marriage certificate, Meri and Reggie were understandably concerned. I explained everything.

"What are you going to do?" Reggie asked.

"I'm going to order a copy online and have it mailed," I said. "I'm not stepping foot back in that place before I get my magic back."

"I could go with you," Meri said. "I think I can still handle that thing."

"I'll just order it online," I said, and that was that.

Chapter Two

No one came into the shop. Not one customer. So, after a while, Reggie and I went upstairs to the apartment and watched a couple of episodes of *The Vampire Diaries*. She loved that show. I couldn't really make fun of her, though. I secretly rewatched the *Twilight* movies when no one was around.

Around lunchtime, we decided to brave the rain and go over to the Brew Station for our free lunch. We ran out to my car, Reggie carried Tangerine like a football and I had Meri tucked in my mostly dried-out bag, and drove around to the other side of the square.

Despite the almost complete lack of customers in the Brew Station, I still didn't feel right taking Tangerine inside, so Meri got dog-sitting duty. The car had a "dog mode" where I could leave the air conditioner and radio on for them. Meri didn't want me going in alone, but he could see me from the car, so he eventually relented.

"You came!" Viv exclaimed as we walked through the doors. "I am so glad to see you guys."

"Slow day, huh?" Reggie said.

"I don't know what it is about this rain and these storms, but it seems to be freaking everyone out," Viv said. "Sometimes rain brings everyone in, but it's really scaring everyone away."

"Yeah, we haven't had anybody in the shop, so we're sort of just closed," I said. "I doubt we'll even go back over there and open up again after lunch."

"I still get paid, right?" Reggie asked.

"Yes, of course," I answered.

"So, are you ladies ready for a feast?" Viv asked. "If you don't mind, I'll just join you."

"Awesome," I said. "You want us to come back and help you get everything ready? We can get our own food."

"Nonsense," Viv said and waved me off. "You guys pick whichever table you want, and I'll be right there."

We took a table away from the window near the counter. Normally, I would have wanted to sit near the window and watch the rain, but I was starting to feel sick of it all. It wasn't like I was wishing for sunshine or anything, but I would have liked a bit of a letup from the unrelenting showers.

That and I was afraid at any moment, the serious thunder and lightning would start again and scare the pants off me. If it did, I'd have to rush out to the car and bring Meri and Tangerine inside.

As if she could read my mind, Viv appeared from the back with a tray of food. "Radar says there's another

41

imbedded storm coming. Why don't you go outside and get those two before it gets here?"

"Are you sure?" I asked.

"It's not like there are any customers in here," she said and looked around. "But if anyone does come in, they can just deal with it. I don't want the critters out there alone when this storm kicks off."

"All right," I said. "I'll grab them."

"I'll help," Reggie added. "I'll grab the doggie."

We rushed outside and went to either side of the car. Reggie grabbed Tangerine from the passenger side, and I reached in and grabbed Meri from the driver's side. We dashed back inside where Viv was setting a paper plate with turkey down for Tangerine and a plate with crumbled bacon for Meri. Both animals happily partook of their meal before settling down at our feet for a snooze.

At least, they tried to relax and take a nap. Just as Viv had said, minutes later another storm came in. The lightning continuously lit up the sky like fireworks were going off above the clouds, and thunder shook the coffee shop.

We ate quickly and without saying much. All of the noise made conversation nearly impossible. I was beginning to feel shell-shocked from the constant pounding and booming.

About halfway through our food, and much to our surprise, customers came tumbling into the shop. It was a man and a young boy, and I could tell right away that the boy had been crying. You could have almost written it off as rain on his face, but I could see his eyes were red and irritated.

He smiled a little, and his face lit up, when he saw Tangerine and Meri.

"Look, dad, a little dog and a kitten," he said to his father. "Can I pet them?" He directed his question at me. Someone had taught him well about asking the owner before you approached a strange animal.

"Sure..." I started to say.

"Stay away from those filthy animals," his father snapped. "What kind of place is this? I should call the police on you and get this restaurant's food license revoked. Where is the manager?"

The little boy sniffled, and his shoulders fell. He just looked so defeated. I sensed that he hoped the animals would lighten his father's mood, and they'd had the opposite effect.

"Dad, please don't," the boy practically whispered.

"Wouldn't matter anyway. Her husband is the sheriff," Reggie snarked at the man, and I watched him bristle.

The little boy's eyes went wide with a look that combined horror and appreciation. My guess was that not many people in his young life had talked to his father that way, but I was worried she would make it worse for him. After all, once they left the Brew Station, there'd be no one for his father to take his anger out on but the boy.

"Stop, Reggie," I whispered under my breath. "Just leave it alone." I nodded my head toward the boy who looked a little terrified.

"Fine," she said and went back to her soup.

"What can I get for you?" Viv asked in her best *please just go away but I'm smiling and being polite* voice. She'd gotten up from the table and gone behind the counter. Evidently, she was just going to ignore his comment about getting her food license taken away. "The specials are on the board. I don't have much else because there hasn't been a lot of business today. Plenty of soup, though, and it's good."

"What is wrong with you?" he spat at her. "Why would you allow animals? You disgust me. Come on, Dixon. We're leaving."

"But I'm hungry," Dixon protested. "The soup smells good. We could eat it back at your house."

The way he said *your house* instead of home told me a lot.

"Shut up," he said and glared at the boy. "What have I told you about begging? Huh? What's wrong with you?"

"Sorry, Dad."

"What, are you going to cry now? Why do you insist on being such a little girl? Huh? Ugh. I swear I should just stop taking you on these stupid weekends. I would, but then your mother would win. She's already ruining you."

Reggie started to stand up, but I put my hand over hers and shook my head, no.

"I'm sorry, Dad. Why don't we go back to your house and I'll make grilled cheese for us," Dixon said. "I can make lunch." He was trying to placate his horrible father, and it broke my heart.

"You're going to cook now? Just like a woman. And you're doing that pathetic thing your mother used to do. Trying so hard to make me happy by assuming you know what I want. You don't, and I wish you'd stop acting like such a wimp," the father snarled at him.

"I'm sorry, I'm sorry." Dixon began to weep in earnest.

"You're disgusting," his father said and raised his hand as if he were about to slap the boy.

I'd tried to get Reggie to back off, but I found myself jumping out of my chair so hard that I knocked it over and sent Meri and Tangerine scrambling. I crossed the room in a few steps and put myself between the man and Dixon.

"You touch him, and I will rip that hand from your body and shove it down your throat," I growled.

"Kinsley!" Viv and Reggie gasped in unison.

But I didn't listen. That man had activated the mama bear in me, and I would not back down.

"Now that's how you act like a man, you little twerp," he said and stepped around me. "Too bad she's a skirt. The town sheriff needs to lay down the law in his own house."

He grabbed Dixon by the back of the neck and practically dragged him outside before I could say anything else. I wanted to follow, but suddenly Viv was there holding me back.

"Don't," she said. "There's nothing you can do that won't cause problems for you and more pain for that little boy."

It made me sick. "There has to be something," I said.

"We'll find out who his mother is," Reggie said. "He was obviously on visitation with his father. The jerk said if he stopped seeing the boy, the mother would win. There's probably a case in family court. You could just smell it. We'll sign sworn statements for her, if she wants them. That's how we can help."

It wasn't good enough, but it had to be. "It's not enough," I said.

"It might save him," Viv said and gave my shoulder a squeeze. "Right now, you guys should get home. There are worse storms coming, and I think I'm going to close up. Unless you guys want to ride it out here?"

"No, we should go," I said as I felt my blood still boiling. I felt like a caged tiger. I had to get out of there even if it was just to drive home. "We've all got basements, right?"

I was significantly calmed by the time I pulled into my driveway. The rain had slowed a bit. It was almost like the eye of the storm, but I knew that was impossible. It was the Midwest, after all. There were derechos and huge lines of thunderstorms, but we did not get hurricanes.

Plus, just as the rain slowed, the weather warnings began to blare from my phone. I took Meri and Tangerine inside and fished some dry sweatpants and a t-shirt out of the dryer.

After I was dressed in dry clothes, I turned on my laptop so I could sit in the kitchen and watch the radar and warnings. I tried to call Thorn and got no answer, so I sent him a text asking him to please call me when he could.

 I made some tea and settled in at the kitchen table to watch the angry red blob on the radar make its way toward Coventry. When my phone finally rang,

I nearly dropped it because my hands were slick with sweat.

"Hey, babe," I said nervously. "Please tell me you are on your way home."

"I can't, Kinsley." Thorn's voice sounded far away due to the wind howling around him. "I'm storm spotting for the county. We've got to make sure that no one is on the roads in the path of danger. I also call it in if... when I see this thing touch down so they can sound the warning system."

"When what touches down?" I asked, but it felt like a dumb question as soon as it crossed my lips. I'd lived in Illinois my entire life, and I knew what was happening. Even without magic, I could feel it in the air and see it in the sickly shade of green sky.

"There's a radar-confirmed tornado nearby, babe. We haven't spotted it, but if the siren goes off, get to the basement. Or just go now... Yeah, just

go now. I'll call you soon, I promise."
Towards the end of his sentence,
Thorn's voice got shaky. I wanted to ask
him what he was seeing, but I knew
keeping him on the phone might put
him in more danger. "I love you," he
finished.

"I love you too," I said. "Call me as soon
as the storm passes."

"I will."

As soon as I was off the phone with
Thorn, I called my mother. While I was
waiting for her to pick up, I went to the
kitchen junk drawer and retrieved an
old flashlight. I pushed the little rubber
button, and it clicked on.

"Thank you," I said to the house. I had
the light on my phone, but it was
always good to have a backup.

"You're welcome," Mom said when she
picked up the phone. "For what,
dear?"

"Sorry, I was thanking the house for the flashlight," I said. "It works."

"I'm glad to hear it. You're okay then?" Mom asked nervously.

"I am, but Thorn is telling me to get down into he basement. At first he said to do it when the sirens went off, but then he sounded all weird and told me to go now."

"Did you listen?" she asked.

"Not yet. I wanted to call you first. This is all so surreal. Like, we should be able to do something about the storm, right? We should be able to dissipate it or reroute it through some unoccupied section of country, right?"

"Normally we would," her voice sounded defeated. "We've tried, sweetie. We've been trying, but we haven't been able to put a dent in it. Well, that's not true. All of us together, we might have lessened the storm some. When it touches down, it might not level Coventry. That's the best we could do considering..."

"I should join in," I said. "I'll go outside and focus every ounce of my power at the sky. We can have everyone in the coven and every friendly witch do the same. Can you put the word out?"

"Kinsley, sweetie, do what Thorn said and go to the basement. We're all going. Take Meri, Tangerine, and some couch cushions to cover your head. Do it now. I'll call you when it's over."

"Okay," I said. "Can you stay on the phone with me?" I suddenly felt small and alone.

"I would, baby, but you need to get the animals and those cushions. Do it fast." There was a panic I'd never heard before rising in her voice. I realized that for the first time in my entire life, my Mom was so scared she couldn't pretend for me anymore. In turn, icy panic gripped my chest. "Go, baby. I love you. Dad loves you."

I wanted to argue, but I was afraid that I'd be putting myself, the baby, and my parents in danger. Not to mention Meri and Tangerine who were counting on me to do the right thing. "Love you too, Mom. I'll text you as soon as we're camped out in the basement."

I slipped the phone into my pocket and set the flashlight down on the kitchen table. When I did, I glanced out the window and saw the clouds. It looked like they were boiling. The wind was so strong, it was bowing the trees over, and tons of limbs were snapping off and flying everywhere.

After snatching the cushions off the sofa, I waddled back into the kitchen, opened the basement door, and chucked them down the stairs. "Meri, get down there," I said. "Go now while I grab Tangerine."

I half expected him to argue with me, but Meri just nodded and darted down the steps. Tangerine was huddled under the kitchen table. I could only imagine that her little doggie storm radar was going nuts. Animals could sense those things long before humans even knew there was a problem.

When I picked up Tangerine, I risked one more glance out the kitchen window. It may have just been my imagination, but I could swear that a few miles off in the distance, I could see something reaching down from the sky. It looked like a dark, gray-blue wedge, and while it didn't seem that dangerous from so far away, my brain knew that something wasn't quite right about what I'd seen.

I held Tangerine tighter, and practically ran down the basement stairs.

Thorn

There was no longer a question that the creek was going to completely cover the road. I was stationed there to make sure it didn't wash anyone away, and I felt fortunate that while I could watch the storm's progression, I wasn't stationed in the path. They'd left that to more experienced members of the county sheriff's office who were also trained storm spotters and veteran storm chasers.

I'd been through the official storm spotter training, but I'd never had any desire to chase them. Of course, now that it was happening, the feeling of being chased by the storms was far worse. It was far better to be the one doing the hunting than to be sitting there waiting to potentially be hunted.

I hadn't seen anyone on the road for a while. A few cars had gone over the bridge and into Coventry when I still felt like it was safe. That had been nearly an hour before. I'd turned away two more cars that I didn't think would make it. The last thing I wanted was to be responsible for people's cars being swept away by the creek that had turned into a raging river. No one would drown on my watch.

In fact, I'd already gotten in my cruiser and moved it back away from the swift water a couple of times. As I was getting ready to get in and move it again, a truck approached.

The driver was a man in his late thirties. He was a big guy in a red and black flannel shirt. He had a full beard, but it was well-maintained. His skin was bronzed from working outside. I was sure that if I checked, I'd find a rifle or a shotgun behind the man's seats, but I wasn't going to check. His demeanor told me he meant me no harm, and while the guy obviously never shied away from a day of hard work, he didn't strike me as the violent type. Just a country boy out doing God-only-knew-what in that storm, but I was about to find out.

"Afternoon, sheriff," he said and gave me a nod.

"This bridge is about to be underwater, sir. I'm going to need you to go back," I said politely. "Whatever it is, it can wait until the storm is over."

"All due respect, sir, it can't," he said, and I saw the raw determination in his eyes.

"What's going on?" I asked and hoped the story was a short one.

"My boy… My stepson, he just called his mama. I promised her I'd get to him. I've gotta get into town and get him. Problems with his father, and I'm afraid if I don't go get the boy, he's going to take off walking in this mess."

"Something I need to get involved in?" I asked. Domestic issues were some of the hardest, and sometimes most dangerous, to deal with.

"No, sir. I think this will be the end of our issues with that man. I assure you I'll call you if we need you, though. Please just let me be on my way. His mama and I can't stomach the idea of him being out in this stuff, but he will. It takes a lot for a little kid to have enough, but I think he's had it."

I knew deep down in the pit of my stomach that the man was going to gun it and go across that bridge no matter what I said. That would have been more dangerous than if I just stepped out of the way and let him go. I didn't know for sure if his truck would make it, but if anyone could, it was him.

"Go on," I said. "Get your boy, but if I have to stand here and watch you get washed away, I'm going to find a way to arrest you."

"Appreciate it, sir," he said and rolled up his window.

I stood back by my car and held my breath as he crossed. The water was at least halfway up his tires, and in some places, it was higher. The truck was heavy enough that he didn't get swept away. We must have had a guardian angel watching over us that day. Him because he didn't die, and me because I doubted I'd be sheriff much longer if I'd let him.

In fact, for a split second, I almost thought I saw a guardian angel standing across the other side of the creek. I blinked and the lady in a white dress with what looked like huge wings tucked behind her back disappeared.

"I'm going to need another vacation after this," I mumbled to myself. "Stress has got me seeing things."

Chapter Three

Kinsley

I'd accidently grabbed one of the throw pillows when I'd yanked the cushions off the couch. It had gotten tossed down the steps with the cushions, and once I'd gotten downstairs, I'd put it underneath an antique oak table stored down there.

That's where I sat with Tangerine on my lap and Meri next to me on the pillow. He was pressed against my leg until thunder shook the house so hard I thought it might have been an earthquake. At that point, he moved onto my lap with Tangerine. The two of them huddled together while I huddled under the table with them.

I couldn't see out into the basement because the table was pushed into a corner, and I'd covered the two remaining openings with the pillows. I'd texted Mom to let her know I was okay and we were ready to ride out the storm. She answered that she and Dad were doing the same.

"The house won't fall on us," Meri tried to reassure me.

"Really? How do you know that?" I asked.

"It's still magical, remember? It can protect us," but he sounded more like he was trying to convince himself than me.

"You can't die," I said. "Remember?"

"I know," he said, but he wasn't worried about himself.

My hands covered my belly protectively. "So why are we even down here if the house will protect us?"

"Because I don't know anything for sure anymore," he said softly and then nuzzled against my stomach. "Better to be too safe."

Before I could say anything else, I heard a rumble off in the distance. It was sort of like thunder, but not quite. If I had to describe it, I would have said it was more like a freight train, and it was getting closer.

"I think it's coming," I said.

"I think you're right," Meri answered.

I put my arms around him and Tangerine and pulled them as close to me as I could. When I closed my eyes, I envisioned a bubble around the house. It might not work. I might not have enough power, but I had to try.

The freight train sound grew closer, and with each passing second, the house above me shook more. For a moment, I wondered if I'd lost my mind and a train really was headed for Hangman's House.

But then, like some sort of miracle, the sound began to get farther away. The house stopped shaking, other than small tremors from the occasional massive clap of thunder, and I decided to crawl out from under the table and check.

I couldn't stay under there forever, and it had grown stiflingly hot. Meri climbed off my lap first, and Tangerine followed. The little dog wasn't shaking anymore either. I trusted her instincts. If she thought the danger had passed, then perhaps it had.

Is it over? I texted to my Mom. Then I sent the same text to Thorn.

My mother answered, but Thorn did not. I was still in the basement at that point, but I was out from under the table. Meri was sitting on the bottom step waiting to go back upstairs like nothing had ever happened. Tangerine sat on the floor below that step watching me and panting happily. Now that the danger had passed, she seemed to think we were just on some weird adventure to the basement.

Yes. It's moved past Coventry. Mom messaged back.

Are you and Dad okay? I'm okay. We're all okay here. Thorn hasn't answered my text. I responded.

He's probably busy, sweetie. I'm sure he'll answer you as soon as he can. She texted, and then my phone rang. It was her, and I guessed she was tired of texting.

"Sorry, I just wanted to talk to you for a second," she said.

"You don't need to apologize," I said. "I'm glad you called. Is your house okay?"

"Your dad is outside checking, but it seems fine. Might be some shingles missing from the roof and some siding that needs to be reattached, but we missed the worst of the damage."

"It's still pouring rain," I said.

"You know your father. He just wants to see for himself that the house is all right. Don't be startled if you look out a window and he's over doing the same at your place," Mom said. "Maybe not, though. When he gets back inside, we're going to go into town and see where we can help. It missed our house, but I know it didn't miss them all."

"That's a good idea," I said. "I'm going to call Viv and Reggie to make sure they are okay. If they are, we can start looking for people that need help. Oh, and Dorian too. I'm sure he'll want to be out documenting all of this."

"Kinsley, just don't overdo it," Mom warned. "And don't do anything to get yourself hurt. Leave the heroics to someone else for now."

"I know, mom. I just want to go see if anyone is trapped in their basements. If

I find anybody, I'll call law enforcement or rescue. I promise I won't try to dig them out myself," I said.

"Well, go on then. I know there's no sense telling you to stay home. Call us when you decide where you're going to start looking. I think your father and I are headed over to some of the new subdivisions. From what I'm hearing from the Aunties, they got hit harder," Mom said.

"Okay, I'll call you when I know," I said.

As soon as I got off the phone with her, I called Reggie, Viv, and Dorian. Viv was heading into the shop because she planned on offering coffee and soup to anyone who needed something to eat or just some comfort.

Fortunately, the rain had slowed to a drizzle by the time I took Tangerine and Meri out to the car. I worried about having Tangerine with me while we searched for survivors, but it felt wrong to leave her alone so soon after the storm. Plus, the severe weather appeared to be clearing, but apparently the atmosphere was still ripe for more.

I arrived at the Brew Station a half hour after I planned. I'd completely forgotten that some of the roads might be difficult or impossible to navigate and had to take several detours to get there.

Dorian and Reggie were waiting there for me drinking coffee and eating soup with a few people who had already found their way there. "Where's Isaac?" I asked when I noticed Dorian was alone at the table. "Is he okay?"

"He's in the back helping Viv. She can cook more food with the help, and he was having a hard time sitting still," Dorian said.

I ate a sandwich and drank some coffee quickly. We hadn't been there long, but the place was like a beacon. People were lining up to get something hot to eat and then talk to their neighbors.

We needed to get out of there and free up a table. Before we left, we talked to people to see which areas of the town were the worst hit. Lots of people talked about the new section of Coventry where my parents had gone, but a few mentioned severe destruction in the neighborhood between where I lived and the new cemetery.

"That's where we should go," I said. "My parents and some of the Aunties are already in the new subdivisions. If they need us, we can join them after we're done in this neighborhood."

Reggie and Dorian agreed. We told Viv where we were going, and she told us to put the word out that people could come into her shop for a meal and a hot cup of coffee. "Tell anyone with kids that there's hot chocolate and cookies. It's on the house."

I teared up a little bit thinking of what she was doing for the community. Isaac was new to Coventry, but he was determined to stay and help her. "We can help more people if I'm here," he said.

As we were leaving, several of her employees showed up to volunteer. The line was out the door, but it began to move faster once she had all hands on deck.

"Should we take my car?" Reggie asked once we were outside.

"It might be better if we walk," I said. "We're all wearing boots, so that's good. I know it's a long walk, but didn't you guys have a hard time driving here?"

"Yeah, I did," Reggie answered.

Dorian said the same.

"I imagine that if that neighborhood was hit hard, it's going to be even worse there," I said. "We don't want your car to end up in the way of the emergency vehicles."

"You're right," Dorian said. "Well, come on. Let's get to hoofing it."

We walked through the square and past the courthouse. I did not look up into the windows because I did not want to see her face that day. It was a distraction I didn't need.

Without looking up, I could still tell that the courthouse was undamaged. The worst of the storm had missed the square. From the outside, I could see that my shop was unharmed as well. I could go inside later and check things out more thoroughly, but it was just stuff. When it came down to it, stuff was unimportant. People were what mattered.

People and pets. Meri was following quietly along as we walked, but we'd left Tangerine back at the Brew Station.

She was in Viv's office in the back of the shop. It was too busy for her to be out front, so Isaac and Viv had promised to check on her as much as they could.

Once we passed the courthouse, we saw a few houses that had some siding ripped off and tree limbs scattered around the yard, but the houses were structurally intact.

A couple of blocks later, and there were houses that were partially destroyed. Some of them had their roofs ripped off while others had large trees collapsed in on them.

As we walked down that street, I tried not to get overwhelmed. What I was seeing was bad, but it might not have been the worst of it. I'd watched the news after EF5 tornadoes, and I needed to be prepared to see sections of Coventry flattened. We didn't know if the storm that hit the town was that bad, but I needed to mentally prepare myself in case it was.

"Kinsley, look," Reggie said and pulled me out of my thoughts.

I looked where she was pointing, and there was an old man sitting on the curb between some debris. He was dirty and had his head in his hands.

"Sir," I called out as we hurried over to him. "Sir, do you need help?"

He slowly lifted his head and looked at me. There was a big scratch over his eye, but other than the dirt, he looked unharmed. "My dog," he barely choked out before descending into sobs. "Shelly…"

"Your dog was in the house?" I said and turned to look at the ruins of his home. It looked as though about a quarter of the house was still standing toward the back, but the rest was either collapsing or had collapsed completely. "Were you in the basement? Was she in the basement with you?"

He took a deep shuddering breath and tried to pull himself together to answer. "She was, but she's an old gal. Shelly's got dementia, and she gets so scared sometimes. She's terrified of things that never used to bother her, so I can't imagine what this storm did to her. Anyway, a window broke while the twister was going through this neighborhood. Made the basement door pop open. She got spooked, ran up the stairs, and into the house. I haven't seen her move that fast in years," he said and sniffled. "Well, you can see the house. I tried to find her, but the roof dang near fell in on me. I want to keep looking, but I've got kids and grandkids who would never forgive me if I died looking for the dog." He began to sob again. "I just hope my son gets here soon. He'll help me. I'd never forgive myself if something happened to her. I'd rather she lived…"

"We'll help you," I said.

"Kinsley," Reggie warned. "You are not going in there. You think of the baby."

"We can walk around the outside and see what we can see," I said. "We can do that."

"Yeah," Reggie said. "Okay, we can do that."

As we started for the house, I heard a soft, muffled whining sound. The man shot up off his place on the curb so fast that Dorian had to keep him from toppling over. "That's her," he said. "Oh, she's alive! Shelly baby, don't worry! Daddy's coming!"

"Please wait here," Dorian gently told the man.

"I can help you," he said defiantly. "I can."

"Let us try," Dorian said. "If you get hurt, it will make it harder for us to save Shelly. Just stay here, and we'll be right back. Please."

The man gave in and agreed to wait. The three of us circled the house as carefully as we could listening for where Shelly's cries came from inside the house. We lucked out, and she seemed to be inside the part that was still standing. That must have been why she survived. I couldn't even think about if she'd gotten confused and wandered into the portion of the structure that was completely collapsed in.

"She's in there," Dorian said as we stood outside the first floor window. The wall was still standing and seemed to be holding up.

"How are we going to get to her?" Reggie asked. "The doors are blocked with collapsed boards."

"I'll climb through this window and hand her out to you guys," Dorian said as he started to roll up his sleeves.

"I should go in," I said. "I'm smaller and I've still got a bit of my powers."

"Absolutely not," Dorian said as he forced the window open. Fortunately, it was either unlocked or the locks were broken. "I'll just be in and out."

Before I could say anything else, he was scrambling up the side of the house and through the window. I heard a thump as he hit the floor inside, and the entire structure shook ominously. Stuff slid from the collapsed parts of the house onto the ground around us.

"Try not to do that again," I called through the window.

"I will do my best," Dorian hollered back sarcastically, but I could hear the tinge of terror in his voice. He was quiet for a couple of seconds and then, "I found her. I'm picking her up and carrying her to the window."

Reggie and I waited at the window for him to return. When he did, it took both of us to get her out of his arms and clear of the house. Shelly was a collie and a sizable one at that. Reggie and I managed to carry her out to the curb where the man waited, without hurting her.

We set her down, and I turned to go back and help Dorian. Just as I did, the house collapsed entirely. Suddenly, someone was screaming.

It was me.

And then Dorian was there gripping my shoulders and shaking me. "I'm all right. I was already out," he tried to soothe me, and I felt my thundering heart begin to slow a fraction.

"I'm sorry. I'm sorry," I said as I tried to get a grip on myself. "I just thought that you…"

"It's okay," Dorian said. "I appreciate that my loss would affect you that deeply."

I punched him in the arm, but his teasing helped me considerably. Reggie was there too rubbing my back.

"No, I'm sorry," said the old man.

"It's okay," I reassured him. "I just freaked out a little. I'm glad we were able to save her. It's good that we came along when we did."

"I think she needs a vet," the old man said. "My car is down the block on top of a neighbor's garage."

Just then, a man across the street came out of his mostly intact house. It was so weird how the tornado had destroyed most of the houses on the block but had left a few relatively untouched. It had no rhyme or reason.

"Mr. Casen?" The neighbor called out. "Is Shelly okay?"

"She needs to go to the vet. I don't have my car," Mr. Casen called back.

"I've got mine," the neighbor said. "Let me pull over there. I heard the vet over on White Oak is open for pets hurt in the storm. If it's not, we'll drive until we find one."

"You'd do that, Tyrone?" Mr. Casen started to cry again.

"Of course I would. Let me get my car."

We helped Tyrone load Shelly into his car, and Dorian helped Mr. Casen into the front seat. I started to believe he was injured somehow the way he was stiffly moving about. He was obviously in pain. His focus was on his Shelly, though, and I figured his injuries weren't life-threatening. He'd get around to seeing a doctor when his dog was safe.

Still, I mentioned what I'd noticed to Tyrone before he got into the car. "I'll keep an eye on him."

With that assurance, they pulled away from the curb, and we continued on our mission to see who we could help.

Chapter Four

A few blocks later, we came across a group of people all standing around the front yard of one particular house. The houses on that block had sustained extensive damage, but none of them appeared to be on the verge of collapse. They had siding stripped off, roofs or sections of walls blown off, and windows broken, but they were still standing.

"What's going on?" I asked as we approached the group.

"We're all here," one woman said. "Everyone on the block is here except the man who lives in this house."

"Who cares?" another woman spat. "I don't know why we are wasting our time on this fool. If the storm took him, it was the Lord's will."

"Beatrice, don't talk like that," the first woman said. "I don't like him either, but we need to see if he's alive. We agreed that the block sticks together."

"That was before he moved in," Beatrice complained. "Olivia, that man is a scourge."

"We don't make exceptions or else we'll start making them for any willy-nilly reason. The block sticks together. That includes Stewart Randell, whether we like it or not," Olivia said.

"Fine, but I'm not going in there after him," Beatrice countered.

"I'll go," Dorian volunteered.

"Oh, no," I said and stuck my arm out to stop him from walking forward. "You're not going into any more houses today that might fall down on you."

"The house looks mostly fine," Dorian protested.

"Yeah, it looks like that from here, but we don't know. The middle could have collapsed or whatever. We don't know why he hasn't come out, but you're not going in."

"Wasn't his kid with him this weekend?" a man in the small crowd asked.

"Oh, he was," Olivia said. "Oh, no."

Dorian shot me a look. "Fine," I said. "Go in."

"I'll go too," the man who had just asked about the kid said. "I'm Herb. Might as well introduce myself if we're going to face death together."

"Dorian," Dorian said and extended his hand to the man. "Let's do this as quickly and safely as we can."

Reggie and I followed them up to the house, but we didn't go in. Instead, we circled around the outside to look in any windows that weren't covered.

We were around the back looking in a dining room window when I saw him. "Dorian, go back outside!" I yelled out.

"What?" I heard him yell back from inside the house.

"He's dead! Go back outside!" I tried again.

He didn't respond that time, but I could only assume he heard me. Of course, what I'd yelled brought all the neighbors around to the window where Reggie and I stood.

They all started taking turns looking as I dialed Thorn's cell phone. My heart thundered in my chest as I waited for him to answer.

"Sorry," he gushed as soon as he picked up. "Some of the cell towers are down, and I just got back to an area with reception. I swear I was going to call you or text you as soon as I wasn't driving."

"It's okay," I said. "I'm glad you're okay, and I love you, but that's not why I'm calling."

"What's going on?"

"Okay, so we were out walking around looking for people who needed help, and we came across a house where a bunch of neighbors said a man was missing in action. Dorian went inside while Reggie and I walked around the outside and looked in the windows. I didn't go in, but I did see a man. His neighbors say his name is Stewart Randell, and he's dead," I said.

"Maybe he was killed in the storm, but I'll head over that way," Thorn responded.

"You might be inclined to think that, but I'm not so sure it was the storm," I said.

"Why do you say that?" Thorn asked.

"Because there's a giant knife sticking out of his back," I said. "And you might need to issue an Amber Alert. His neighbors say his son was with him, and so far I haven't seen a kid. Should we go upstairs in the house and look?"

"No," Thorn said quickly. "I'll do that when I get there."

After people got done looking in the window at Stewart's body, they walked back up to the front of the house. I was waiting up there for Thorn, and they all sort of congregated around me even though no one was saying anything.

"You guys know that the Brew Station is open right now, right? Viv is there giving out soup and coffee for anyone who wants to eat or just wants some company," I finally said.

"Maybe we should all head over that way," Olivia said. "I don't think we're going to do any good here. Maybe we'd all feel better with some hot food and coffee."

"What about the boy? They might need us to help look for him," someone said.

"I'll call Viv and let her know if there's going to be a search for the boy," I said. "Until we know for sure that's necessary, why not go get something to eat?"

There probably wasn't going to be anywhere for any of them to sit once they did get food and coffee, but at least the rain had stopped. It was a bit chilly outside, but at least it wasn't cold. Perhaps Amelda would let people into the library to eat and warm up. I knew she was a stickler for the rules about eating and drinking in the library, but it was an exceptional circumstance.

I sent her a text asking her if she'd consider it.

Already on it. Was her reply. I should have known she would do everything she could to take care of the people in her town.

Reggie, Dorian, and I waited outside on the front sidewalk while Thorn combed the house looking for the man's son. At first when he came out, I couldn't read his expression, but then the corners of his mouth pulled into a soft, reassuring smile.

By that time, there were other deputies there. They'd all had to stop what they were doing and come to the scene, so Thorn went to speak with them. The three of us overheard the news, though, as he told it to Jeremy.

"There's no child in the house," he said.

"I'm going to call the kid's mom, and then if she doesn't know where he is, we'll issue an Amber Alert," Jeremy responded.

"We should have had the neighbors stay," I said. "They'd know who to call."

"Oh, we know who to call," Jeremy said softly. "We've had to deal with Mr. Randell before. He's in our system."

I knew that we should leave, but I couldn't until after Thorn called the child's mother. Jeremy's words about how Mr. Randell was in their system haunted me.

"Dixon is fine," Thorn said when he hung up the phone. "His stepfather picked him up just before the storm."

"You said Dixon?" I asked Thorn.

"Yeah, why?" He cocked one eyebrow up when he asked.

That was when it hit me that I recognized the dead man. He was the one that had come into the Brew Station before the tornado. Dixon was the little boy with him who he'd treated so terribly.

"We saw them before the storm at the Brew Station. It was really close to the time the tornado hit. He was just being awful to that boy," I said.

Jeremy was writing down what I said. "And you can confirm this?" he asked Reggie and Dorian.

"I can," Reggie said. "I saw it all, and so did Viv."

"Not me," Dorian replied. "I wasn't at the coffee shop until later."

"Why don't you guys head over to the Brew Station and let the neighbors know the boy is okay," Thorn said. "I'll be along when we're done with the scene to speak with Viv about her statement."

"We should keep looking," I protested. "We need to keep searching for people who need help."

"No," Thorn said softly. "Thank you for what you've done, but search and rescue is on their way here. The National Guard is coming as well. Red

Cross is setting up in the square for now while they find temporary shelter for people who are displaced. You need to stay out of danger, and stay out of their way."

"Come on," Reggie said when she sensed me bristling. "Let's go talk to the neighbors. We can find out why they hated this guy so much."

"Reggie," Jeremy warned. "Stay out of this."

"No harm in having a conversation with some neighbors. It's just gossip after all. Surely, there is no law against gossip, right?"

"Not in this town," Dorian said.

It took us a while to walk back to the Brew Station, but at least the rain held out. The sun didn't come out, but we stayed dry. As much as I hated myself for it, I started to block out the devastation on our way back. My mind and heart were overwhelmed, and my body had begun to follow.

Exhaustion gripped me in a way I hadn't expected. My body felt heavy, and that was especially true of my legs and belly. I wasn't in pain, but my stomach felt like a cannon ball. It was as if some sort of shift had taken place. Gravity pulled at me, but intuitively, I knew not to be scared. It was just... heavy.

Upon arriving at the square, we found Stewart's neighbors sitting at a table set up outside of the Brew Station. I wasn't sure where the tables had come from, but someone must have donated them to give patrons a place to sit. There were also people heading over to the library with bags and coffee cups in their hands.

We went inside the Brew Station to get some hot coffee, and I needed something to eat. At least I thought I did. I was at that point where I couldn't figure out if I was starving or sick to my stomach. Since I felt a bit lightheaded too, I decided to eat something.

While we stood in line, I watched out the window. A few minutes after we arrived at Viv's place, trucks started to roll into town. In addition to the Red Cross and National Guard trucks, there were various search and rescue vehicles too.

"Were we the only ones who got hit?" I asked. "This seems like a lot of help."

"I think we are," Reggie said. "I think the twister spared most of the towns around us. Coventry's luck finally ran out."

"I think we're lucky," Dorian said. "One death so far. It could have been so much worse."

"You're right," I agreed. "We are fortunate and even more so that we have this much help coming in. I guess things are worse than I thought, though." Even as I said it, a few more National Guard trucks rumbled by.

A couple of minutes later, it was our turn at the counter. Viv smiled at us, but you could tell she was frazzled. "How'd it go, guys?" She looked grateful to have a moment to stop running around and chat.

"You've heard that we found someone, right?" I asked. I thought for sure someone would have said something by then, but perhaps the neighbors hadn't.

"I did, but I didn't want to bring it up if you didn't want to talk about it," she said.

"Dorian almost died saving a dog," I said because I wasn't sure if I wanted to talk about it or not.

"I was fine," Dorian interjected. "You worry too much."

"Is the dog okay?" Viv asked.

"The man and his neighbor took her to the vet, but I'm pretty sure she was going to be okay," I said. "She was an old girl with dementia who got spooked during the storm, but she managed to escape into a part of the house that didn't collapse."

"Oh, that's good," Viv said and pressed her palm to her chest.

"The man we found had a son," I said. "He wasn't in the house. He was missing. But, it's okay."

"He's with his mother," Viv said. "Right?

How do you know that?" I was genuinely impressed and curious.

"The man's neighbors were here. One of them found the man's ex-wife's phone number in her purse. It was on an old scrap of paper, and she'd completely forgotten about it until today. Anyway, she called the ex-wife and the boy was with her. The kid's stepfather went to pick him up before the worst of the storm."

"Yeah. That's the version I heard too," I said. "Thorn confirmed it before I headed over here."

"We compared notes, and, Kinsley, I think the dead man and his son were that man and the boy, Dixon, who were here before the tornado hit," Viv said.

"Well, it makes sense why he called his stepdad to pick him up if that is the case," I responded.

"I've got a line forming," Viv said after that.

I looked behind me and several dozen more people had showed up at the Brew Station. "I'll call you soon," I said. "But call me sooner if you need anything."

Viv got our orders, and the three of us headed out of the coffee shop. There were too many people waiting for tables or a place to sit for us to stay there. It wouldn't have felt right.

Instead, Dorian, Reggie, and I headed over to the apartment above the shop. Dorian's old place made a good resting spot where we could still be close to the action. Tangerine stayed with Viv for the time being. Meri followed us across the street and curled up on Dorian's old sofa as soon as we were inside.

We sat around him in the living room eating our food quietly. That was until I reached out my hand to grab my coffee and it jumped away from me.

"Whoa," Dorian said as his hand shot out to catch it before it spilled all over the coffee table and our food.

"Nice reflexes," Reggie said before taking another bite of her sandwich.

"What just happened there?" Dorian asked.

"I don't know," I said.

I stared at my hand in shock. A voice in the back of my mind whispered to me that it was a burst of magic, but I ignored it. There was no way that uncontrolled magic just shot out of my hand.

Right?

"You just knocked the cup over," Reggie said. "What is wrong with you two? You both look like you've seen a ghost."

"I've had it happen before, but it was when I was a teenager. It was before I studied hard enough to control my power," I said.

"Well, there you go," Reggie said and put her sandwich down on the table. "If it happened when you were a teenager and it's happening now, then it's a hormone thing. It's because you're pregnant. Just chill out."

"I've been pregnant for a while," I said. "This magical weirdness is all new."

"Then you probably moved into a different part of pregnancy or something. It's a shift, right?" she said.

"What part of pregnancy is that?" I asked skeptically.

"Dude, I don't know anything about witch pregnancies," Reggie said.

She picked up her sandwich and started eating again after that. By that point, Dorian had stood up and walked to the window. He was watching the National Guard set up a base on one side of the square and the Red Cross do the same on the other.

"I should be down there covering this," he said so softly I nearly didn't hear him.

"You should go," I said in response.

"Not if you're going to go back out there. I'm not leaving you alone and in danger," Dorian said.

"Well, look at you trying to go all alpha male on us," Reggie said with a chuckle.

"I'm not," Dorian said and blushed. "I just..."

"It's okay," I interrupted. "You can go do your job, though. Reggie and I aren't going to go looking for more survivors or anything like that. We'll stay out of the way of the National Guard."

"You swear?" Dorian asked.

"Cross my heart," I said.

Chapter Five

I didn't lie to him. Reggie and I didn't go back out into Coventry looking for survivors.

We didn't go home either.

"There's going to be no time for them to investigate the murder," Reggie said as soon as Dorian was gone. "Jeremy and Thorn aren't going to be able to use any resources to solve it, and we know that the first couple of days of the investigation are the most important part."

"We shouldn't," I said, but there was no conviction behind my words.

"We won't do anything that will get us in trouble," she said.

"Yeah, right," I retorted with a chuckle. "I know you better than that."

"There's no law against us going to talk to the ex-wife," Reggie said.

"I'm pretty sure if it interferes with a homicide investigation, there's probably a law or two against it," I said.

"We're not going to interfere, and since when do you care?" Reggie asked.

"Since I promised both my husband and Jeremy that I wouldn't put myself in any danger," I said. "I'm trying to stick to my word."

"We're not going to be in any danger," Reggie said. "We're just going to have a conversation. There won't even be any breaking and entering. If anyone knows who might have wanted that man dead, I'm betting on his ex-wife."

"I don't know," I said.

"If she was married to an abusive man, she's far more likely to talk to us than to Thorn or Jeremy. We'd actually be doing them a favor," Reggie said.

And just like that, we were in the car headed for the address Reggie found on the internet. Apparently, Dorian had a subscription to some website where you could get people's addresses and phone numbers, and Reggie had swiped the login. It was supposed to be used by members of the press and private investigators, but that didn't stop Reggie.

There was water everywhere as we drove to the address outside of Coventry. For a while, I thought we might not make it all the way there. The fields on either side of the road were flooded all the way up to the shoulder. It looked like we were driving across a road right down the middle of a massive lake. It was unnerving, to say the least.

The bridge we had to cross wasn't washed out, though, and it looked to still be in good shape. The water level in the creek below it had fallen to the point where there was a few feet of clearance, so I decided it was safe and drove across.

"This is so strange," Reggie said as we turned onto the road where Melanie Parker lived with her son, Dixon, and husband, John. I only knew his name because it was listed in the database where Reggie had gotten the address.

"What we're doing?" I asked as I slowed down. The GPS had alerted me that we were arriving at our destination.

"No, the water everywhere. I can't remember ever seeing flooding like this. It's like some massive ocean decided to swallow us up," she said.

"It is unnerving," I said.

We pulled into the driveway of a small, white farmhouse. It looked virtually untouched by the storm, and I couldn't help but think the tornado really had targeted Coventry. That was a silly thought, though. Nature was a wild thing. It had no intent. We'd just happened to be in the path of its occasional fury.

Reggie and I made our way across the sidewalk and then up the front steps. For a brief second before I knocked, I considered turning around and going back to the car.

I swallowed my apprehension and knocked anyway. I wasn't going to hurt anyone with my misbehaving magic, but I did need to go back to the basics. I'd have to relearn the techniques I'd used to manage it when I was a teenager. I had to start over again.

A few seconds after I knocked, a woman cracked the door open and peeked out. She had bright blue eyes and long, chestnut hair.

"Can I help you?" she asked.

"My name is Kinsley Skeenbauer, and this is my friend Reggie. We wanted to talk to you about your ex-husband," I said.

"I already told the sheriff when he called that Dixon is here," she said warily. "But we didn't kidnap him, if that's what my good-for-nothing ex is saying. I know that it's his visitation time, but Dixon was threatening to walk off... into that storm. I had to send John to pick him up. I'll be happy to tell the judge all about it."

"I understand," I said softly. "I... I'm not with the sheriff's office or the court. Can we please come in and talk to you for a few minutes?"

She studied me for a second and then opened the door wider to beckon us inside. "I was just making coffee. Would you ladies like a cup?"

"If it's not too much trouble," I said.

"Not at all," Melanie said as we walked into a living room area. "Have a seat, and I'll be right back."

There was a blue armchair, matching blue sofa, and a brown recliner. Reggie and I sat down on either side of the sofa and waited silently for Melanie to return.

She came back a few minutes later with three mismatched mugs on a pine tray. There was also a blue plastic sugar container and a thing of powdered coffee creamer.

"Hang on, I've got cookies too," she said after setting the tray down. I'd thought I'd smelled the scent of fresh baked chocolate chip cookies when we'd entered the house. Melanie came back a minute later with a plate full of them. "They are Dixon's favorite. I figured it would cheer him up, but I always bake way too many."

I was hesitant at first to take any of the cookies given that we were there to pry into her life with her ex, but they smelled too good to resist.

"Thank you," I said and took two.

Reggie did the same.

"So, what are you ladies really here for?" Melanie said and looked at us with eyes that could pierce lead. She'd been through some things, and while it hadn't dulled the light in her eyes, there was a worldly weariness around the edges.

"I don't know if the sheriff's department in Coventry told you about your ex-husband," I said.

"They called here about Dixon, but no one told me about anything having to do with Stewart. They just said they couldn't find Dixon, and I figured Stewart was up to his old tricks. Legally, Dixon can't leave his visitation with his father unless his life is in danger. He's getting older now, though, and has a mind of his own. A couple of times we've had to pick him up because he threatened to take off walking if someone didn't get him. Stewart, of course, dragged me to court to have me fined or arrested. So far he hasn't been successful, but you can tell the judge doesn't like women. He's getting to the point where he said he will find me in contempt if I don't find a way to control Dixon. As if that's ever going to make Dixon love Stewart again," she said and let out an exasperated snort. "I've tried to warn Stewart that he's ruining his relationship with Dixon forever, but he doesn't listen. All he cares about is control and getting his way. As sad as it is to say, he doesn't care whether Dixon loves him or not."

"I understand," I said as gently as I could. Nothing she'd said was a shock given what I'd witnessed at the Brew Station between Stewart and his son.

"Well, look at me just blabbering away. Guess I've told you my whole life story now," Melanie said and looked down at the floor.

"It's okay. We have that effect on people," Reggie said and shoved half a cookie into her mouth.

"Who are you guys again? I mean... why are you here?" Melanie asked.

"I guess we should just tell you," I began. "The sheriff that called you, Thorn, is my husband. I guess he probably wanted to tell you about Stewart in person, but I don't know when he'll have time to get out here to do it. Coventry was hit by a tornado, and things are a mess."

"Tell me what about Stewart?" Melanie asked. "What's going on?"

"He was killed," I said. "The only reason I know that is because I was out helping look for survivors in some of the houses that were destroyed. I found him dead in his kitchen. That's the reason the sheriff was looking for Dixon. The neighbors thought he was supposed to be with Stewart, and everybody panicked when we couldn't find him."

"Stewart's dead?" Melanie asked and then held her breath.

"He is," I said. "He was for sure dead."

She let out her breath, and I could have sworn the corners of her lips played up into the tiniest smile. If nothing else, she looked relieved.

"He was probably murdered," Reggie added, and I elbowed her in the side. I'd intended to find a more delicate way to say that part.

"That's why we're here," I said. "I was hoping you could tell us who might have wanted him dead."

"Besides me?" Melanie asked with an awkward chuckle. "I thought you said that your husband was the sheriff. Do you work for him?"

"I don't," I said. "I was just hoping you might talk to us about it. My husband and his deputies are swamped right now. I wanted to help."

"I think our conversation is done," Melanie said and stood up. "Thank you ladies for coming by and giving me the news, but I'm going to have to call my lawyer before I talk to anyone about this."

That was our cue to leave, and I could see in her eyes she had no intention of backing down. "Come on, Reggie. Let's go," I said. "Thank you so much for the coffee and the cookies."

"Thank you for..." Melanie searched for the right words, "changing my life."

Chapter Six

When we got outside, Reggie and I found Dixon on the large front porch playing with Meri. The boy had a string tied to a stick, and Meri was going along with chasing it as Dixon let it dip down and then yanked it away.

"Hey there. I thought he was in the car," I said.

"He talks," Dixon said without looking at me. He was still intently playing with Meri.

"He's a cat. He doesn't talk," I lied.

"Yes, he does. I heard him. I heard him talking to himself in your car. That's why I let him out. I hope you don't mind, but I was worried he'd gone bonkers."

We were outside of Coventry, so the supernatural veil that kept people from noticing our magic was thin. It was nearly threadbare when it came to children anyway. So many of them could see right through it, but adults didn't believe them. It didn't really have to work on them because when they told people what they saw, the grownups thought they were making up silly stories.

"Well, I have to take him home now. Thank you for keeping him company. I'm sure he appreciates it," I said.

"My dad's dead, isn't he?" Dixon said without missing a beat.

"I…"

"I heard you talking to my mom," Dixon said and stopped moving the string. Meri looked defeated.

"You hear a lot," Reggie said.

"I do," Dixon said without further comment.

"I'm sorry you had to hear the news that way," I said.

"I'm not," Dixon said. "I mean, I never wished he was dead or anything, but now I don't have to be afraid anymore."

"I'm glad that you don't have to be afraid anymore," I said. "I'm sorry that it took this for you to feel safe."

"Miss Olivia said that if he ever hurt me again, she would kill him herself," Dixon said as he knelt to scratch Meri under the chin. "Maybe now that I don't have to go to dad's house anymore, I can get a kitten of my own. I will be able to take care of it all of the time."

"That's not the reason I wouldn't let you have another kitten," Melanie had opened the front door and was standing there listening. She'd been as quiet as a mouse, and I hadn't heard her. "I don't mind helping you take care of a cat. That's not why..."

"Dad killed the cat we had before mom and I left him" Dixon said matter-of-factly. "Even mom said that's not what happened, but I know."

"Dixon come inside, sweetie. We can talk about getting you another kitten, okay?" Melanie shot us a look.

I grabbed Reggie's arm and pulled her down the steps. I was pretty sure she was angry with her dead ex and not us, but it was me and Reggie that were in her sights. I knew better than to stand around waiting in the path of a mama bear about to charge.

"Hey," Reggie protested.

"Come on, we need to go."

Chapter Seven

"You don't really think Olivia killed her neighbor, do you?" Reggie asked as we drove back toward Coventry.

"I don't want to believe it, but I don't know her well enough one way or another," I said.

"We're going to talk to her, aren't we?" Reggie asked.

"Do you have somewhere else you have to be?"

"We should go check on the shop," she offered.

"Well, that gives us a good reason to be back in the square. We'll check around for Olivia first, and then we'll go to the shop," I said.

"Do you really think she's still there?"

"If she's not, then we can find out where she went. Was her house okay?

Or do you think she had to go to the shelter?" I asked.

"I can't remember," Reggie said. "All of that is kind of a blur."

"Maybe they are all still hanging out at the Brew Station," I said. "That will make things easier."

"It's only been an hour," Reggie added. "They might still be there. Or over at the library."

And then I got a cramp.

Except it was unlike any cramp I'd ever experienced in my life. My entire abdomen seized like I'd been hit with an electrical current, and I nearly fell over.

"Are you okay?" Reggie asked as she instinctively shot out an arm to steady me.

Water pooled at my feet.

"I think my water just broke," I said with a nervous chuckle. "Either that or I peed myself."

"That's impossible, Kinsley. You're not due for a couple of months," Reggie said as her eyes went wide with horror.

"Well, you tell the baby that, and she'll get back to you about her schedule," I said with another nervous chuckle. My attempts to keep things lighthearted and prevent myself from panicking were making me sound deranged.

"What do I do? Where do we go? I should call your mother," Reggie said. "Aren't you doing this at home? We should go there."

"Well, given that this isn't supposed to be happening and also the state of magic lately, I'd say the hospital," I answered. "Something's off, and I need to go to the hospital."

Before Reggie could say anything, the tornado sirens went off again. Just under the blaring sound of the sirens, I could hear my phone ring.

Again...

I couldn't remember hearing them before. I told myself it was because the tornado was too loud, but I didn't know.

In the middle of that thought, another contraction hit me like a train. My knees buckled, and I almost fell over. Reggie held me up until it was over.

"I need to call Thorn," I said.

"You need to get in the car. I'll call Thorn and tell him to meet us there," Reggie said.

I wanted to argue, but I didn't feel right. My stomach felt like a sinking stone, but my head was light. My pulse pounded in my temples, but it felt like it was a million miles away.

"Something isn't right," I said softly as Reggie waited for Thorn to pick up.

"Thorn, she's in labor. Something's wrong. I'm taking her to the hospital. You have to meet us there," Reggie said and then was silent for a moment. "No. Absolutely not. I can handle it."

"What is it?" I asked, but she just patted my arm.

"Okay fine," Reggie said. "Fine. I'm serious, Thorn. I promise I'll wait," she said and then hung up.

"What's going on?" I asked. My head was swimming and the siren felt like it was drifting away.

"Thorn said the sirens are going off prematurely. They just got them back online. Apparently, there was a glitch or something. Whatever. Anyway, there is a tornado, and it is close. The storm is moving into a position between here and the hospital. He said he'd be here as fast as he could, and he's driving you there."

"Reggie, I don't feel very good," I said and crumpled to the curb.

My pants were already wet, so I didn't mind sitting on the damp pavement. The fact that my feet were in a puddle several inches deep wasn't exactly pleasant, but since I was at least sitting down, I didn't mind.

"Let's get you up," Reggie said.

She started tugging under my arms trying to help me stand. "No, I want to sit for a while. I'll get up when Thorn gets here."

Reggie tried to lift me again, but I didn't move. "I should have called an ambulance," she said.

"Thorn will get here faster," I said.

"Do you have any healing magic you can use?" Reggie whispered to me. "Anything at all?"

"I can't," I said. I felt so drained, and then another contraction hit me. All I could do was grip my belly and try not to scream too loudly. We'd already attracted a small crowd. "Meri," I said.

He came sprinting down the street. Apparently, he'd wandered off to investigate something. Probably trying to figure out how close the tornado was. That's what I told myself.

Wordlessly, he pressed himself against my back. The pain lessened a bit, and I felt strong enough to stand up.

As Reggie helped me to my feet, Thorn's cruiser pulled up and its tires squealed to a stop. "Get her in," he shouted when he was halfway out of the car.

He rushed around and helped Reggie get me in the car. As soon as they had my feet inside, Thorn buckled the seatbelt across me.

"I'm coming with you," Reggie said.

"No, it's too dangerous. Just go home and get to your shelter. The storm is still possibly coming in this direction. You can come to the hospital after it passes," he said and shut my door.

I looked out the window, and Reggie was standing there looking at me. She contemplated it for a few seconds before nodding her head and taking off for her car. I noticed that the sirens had stopped, but the sky was turning an inky shade of black.

"We shouldn't be going anywhere," I said as I stroked Meri's fur. He'd managed to jump into my lap before Thorn shut the door.

"I know that," Thorn said. "But looking at you, I can see that we have to try."

"We could stay here and call my family. Call the coven together," I said. "Maybe together they can..."

"No," Thorn said as he pulled away from the curb. "Maybe before the magic went wonky, but no. Not now. I can't put you in the hands of... It's just that there might not be enough magic..."

"To save me?" I asked. Suddenly, I wished the cruiser had a vanity mirror. "Do I look that bad?"

"You just look like you don't feel well, sweetie," Thorn said. He squeezed my hand, but his eyes didn't meet mine.

We drove out of Coventry and off toward the hospital. The rain kicked in again, but at least some of the flooding had partially receded.

"We don't have to cross any bridges, Well, one, but that one's not close to the water. We'll be all right," he said as if he'd read my thoughts. "At least in that respect."

I wanted to ask him what he meant, but I already knew. The sky was as black as night, and it looked like it was boiling. Hairs on the back of my neck stood at attention, and I knew we were in a bad place.

Thorn hit the gas and began to drive much faster than I ever would have expected him to go with me in the car. When I turned to look out my window, I saw why.

Off in the distance, I couldn't tell exactly how far, was a tornado. The wedge was a sinister scene, and it was so close to us. Too close for me to feel safe.

"Thorn," I choked out.

"I know, sweetie. I know. Hold on," Thorn replied.

"Should we turn around? Should we go back? I don't know if you should try to outrun it," I said.

"It's not heading right for us," he said. "I can make it."

I was about to argue when another wave of contractions hit me. I squeezed my eyes shut and prayed to the Goddess.

By the time I opened them, we had passed the tornado. As long as it didn't change directions, we were in the clear.

"We should be there in about five minutes," Thorn said as we drove into the city. "I'll call ahead and let them know we're on our way."

His words sounded far away. The sky was still bubbling and black above us, but there didn't seem to be any tornadoes. The rain wasn't very heavy either. I recalled reading somewhere about dry super cells, but the memory was as fuzzy as the rest of my thoughts.

The pain was nearly unbearable, and somehow, on the short trip to the next town, the contractions had accelerated. They felt as though they were right on top of each other. I couldn't catch my breath. All I wanted was a few seconds of rest.

But more than that, I was worried about my baby. If I wasn't getting enough oxygen, then she wasn't either. I tried to tell myself I was just panicking, but it really did feel like I couldn't fill my lungs all the way.

"Kinsley?" I heard the terror in Thorn's voice as we pulled up under the awning that covered the emergency room doors. "Kinsley, sweetie? We're here. Baby, please," Thorn pleaded as he squeezed my hand.

I wanted to answer him, but I just couldn't. Suddenly, a rush of people came out of the automatic doors. People in scrubs and white coats with serious faces. Thorn opened my car door, and I felt myself being dragged out.

If a situation could be calm and frantic at the same time, that's how I would have described it. There was a flurry of activity, but everyone around me was studious and professional.

Words about hypoxia and oxygen saturation swirled around me. Thorn was nearby at first, and I could tell he was on the phone with my mother.

"Brighton, you have to wait until the storm passes," he said. "She's here in good hands now, but you won't be doing anyone any favors if you get killed trying to drive through that storm. Give it twenty minutes to pass and then you can come. The doctors will take care of her."

"Meri," I cried out as I looked back and watched the doors close with him on the other side of them. A nurse had shooed him out.

Thorn locked eyes with me and gave me a nod. He'd find a way to sneak him inside. I had to have Meri with me. I just had to have him there.

I was on a gurney being rolled somewhere. Bright lights above blocked my vision as they poked and prodded me. But it was all some sort of weird fever dream. I couldn't hold onto a thought for more than a few seconds. I kept reaching for Meri, and then remembering that he wasn't there.

A nurse leaned over me talking about informed consent. Could I sign a form for a procedure? *What procedure?* I thought. I was having a baby. What procedure could I possibly need?

Next thing I knew, Thorn was in the room. He told her that he was my husband. He signed the form.

They'd put an IV in my hand as soon as I'd come in. I felt that part as clear as day. Once Thorn signed the form, someone injected something into it. The medicine was icy at first, but then it burned and stung as it snaked up the vein in my arm.

At some point, though, it started to make the fuzzy edges even fuzzier. I was transported away to a place that wasn't sterile and antiseptic. When they wheeled the gurney down the hall toward giant double doors, I could have sworn I was floating away on a bed of clouds.

We passed through the doors, and someone put an oxygen mask over my face. A blue cloth was hung right below my chest, and I tried to squeeze Thorn's hand. But he wasn't there. In the movies, the husband was always there.

Instead a nurse grabbed my hand and gave it a squeeze. "He can't be in here," she said as if she could read my mind. As if she'd done this a million times.

That made me feel better.

Then I was dreaming.

Chapter Eight

I woke up to the sound of squalling. There was a baby nearby, and the little guy, or girl, had a set of lungs on them.

"Kinsley," I heard a familiar voice say. "Look at that," the voice cooed. "Mommy's awake."

"Mommy's awake?" I asked groggily. I tried to sit up, but pain in my guts made me wince.

Where was I?

It started to come back to me just as Thorn stepped up to the side of the hospital bed I found myself tucked into. He had a little bundle in his arms. A little bundle wrapped in a pink blanket with an even pinker stocking cap on her tiny head. Little fists popped out of the blanket and swung around clumsily in the air.

"I'm really bad at swaddling her," he admitted. "I was hoping the nurse would come back and do it again."

"My baby..." I said as if the whole thing was a dream. It still seemed like one. "Is that our baby?"

"She most certainly is," Thorn said. "Do you feel up to holding her? I think that would be good, but only if you're up for it."

"How long have I been out?" I asked as I fought through the pain and tried to sit up.

"Hold on, sweetie. Let me help you with that." Thorn held the baby in one arm and used a little control box on the siderail to raise the head of the bed for me. "Let me know when to stop."

"That's good," I said when he got to a point where I felt upright but not too upright. "Yes, please let me hold her."

Thorn put the little bundle in my arms, and the squalling instantly stopped. The baby nuzzled against my chest, and her eyes got heavy.

"There," Thorn said with a sigh. "It's exactly what she needed."

"Her eyes are blue," I said. "I know that lots of babies are born with blue eyes and they change, but hers are really, really blue."

"That's not all," Thorn said. "Look at this."

He pulled off her little stocking cap, and a full head of blonde curls sprang free. She had his eyes and his hair. There was no denying it, but it was so strange. Had magic somehow changed things...

Before I could say anything, the door to the room opened and my mother and Lilith came bursting through. They both rushed over to the bed and threw their arms around me.

"Everyone else would be here, but for some reason, the hospital said only two more visitors," Mom said as she squeezed me until I squeaked.

"Oh, now, Brighton, be careful. You're going to split her open," Lilith said. "She probably needs another hit of the good juice. Has anyone showed you how this works?"

Lilith held up a small wand connected by a tube to my IV. On the end was a bright red button.

"Not yet," Thorn said. "She just woke up."

"Allow me to demonstrate," Lilith said and pushed the button.

As sweet, warm pain relief washed over me, she cackled.

"Morphine," Mom said. "You push the button when you need it, but there's a limit. It will make a soft clicking sound if you push it and you can't have more yet. Obviously by the look on your face, you'll be able to tell when you get a dose."

"That's nice," I said as the pain in my abdomen melted away.

"So, you have a lot of explaining to do," Lilith said with a wink.

"What do you mean?" I asked.

"Well, we were under the impression that your husband was going to be raising another man's child. It was one of the more interesting scandals to hit Coventry, and now look at what you've done. How can we all be scandalized if it's his baby?"

"And how?" Mom asked. "I didn't think it was possible myself, but the likeness is undeniable."

"And the lack of likeness to a certain someone else," Thorn said gently. "But like Kinsley said earlier, sometimes babies are born with blue eyes and they change later."

"That child is not half vampire," Lilith said with a huff. "I can tell you that for certain."

Just then, something under my covers stirred. It alarmed me at first, but then I laughed when Meri's head popped out from under the blankets.

"We didn't wake you, did we?" I asked.

"It's hard to get a good night's sleep around here," he said as he climbed out from under the blanket and lay down next to my hip.

"You're not going to shrug us off," Lilith said. "Explain yourself. Explain how you've managed the boring task of having your husband's child."

"She is early," Mom said. "Unless she's not..."

Thorn and I looked at each other. He smiled at me again, and there was so much pride and joy in his eyes, I could barely believe that it could be true.

"Well, there was this one time..." I started to say.

"Oh, I knew it!" Lilith said and clapped her hands together. "Do go on, please."

"Well, we didn't know for sure," I said.

"What?" Mom asked and cocked her head to one side. "Could you elaborate without going into more detail than what your mother needs to hear?"

"Well, it was back when Thorn and I were having some problems getting along. We got into a big fight. He stormed out, was gone for a couple of hours, and then he came back so we could yell at each other some more. Eventually, we realized how dumb we were being, but by that time, he'd drunk a six-pack of his favorite beer, and I was pretty deep into a bottle of wine," I said. "I think we made up."

"We woke up the next morning next to each other in bed, but our clothes were on," Thorn said.

"But they looked like a monkey had dressed us in the dark," I added.

"So, we didn't know, and we decided not to talk about it," he said.

"I thought it would be better if we didn't discuss it again because you both know how Thorn feels about things like that before marriage. We just left it alone," I said.

"Like I said," Meri snarked, "all it takes is once."

"So, the baby is Thorn's," Mom said with a smile. "This is wonderful."

"It is," Thorn added. "I can't believe it myself, and I would have been over the moon with her either way, but this is just so much more than I ever could have hoped for."

I reached out and took his hand with mine. "We should name her so we can stop calling her the baby," I said. "Did you have anything in mind? We didn't get around to picking anything yet."

"You should name her," Thorn insisted. "You and your family."

"No," I said and squeezed his hand. "She's your little miracle. You should name your firstborn."

"I can't get the name Laney out of my mind," he said. "It's been floating around in there ever since the doc handed her to me the first time."

"Laney?" I said.

"You don't like it?" Thorn asked. "Like I said, you and your family can choose."

"No, I love it. It suits her perfectly," I said.

"It really does," my mom agreed as she slipped Laney's stocking cap back on over her curls.

"I'm surprised I wasn't showing more, because she's not a tiny baby," I said. "She's big and healthy."

"The doctor said something about your parts being tipped in there," Thorn said and blushed furiously. "I didn't catch it all, but he said that whatever it was, it made women show less."

Later that evening when my mother and Lilith had gone back to Coventry for the night, it was just my little family left in the hospital room. Thorn sat in a chair next to the bed, and Laney slept against my chest. Meri snuggled against my feet, and so far, none of the nurses had acknowledged his presence.

I'd been out of bed once when a kindly nurse had helped me take a shower while Thorn held me up and kept my IV site dry. It had been quite the affair, but I felt so much better. A nice hot shower could fix a lot of things.

"Can't he heal you?" Thorn asked when I finally gave up flipping through the television channels.

"He has as much as he could," I said. "That's why I was able to shower today instead of tomorrow, but there's only so much we can do now. I want him to save his magic for Laney."

Thorn looked like he was about to argue, but he just nodded in agreement. "Are you okay? Can I get you anything?"

"That last nurse said they had grape popsicles at the nurse's station," I said and Thorn sprung out of his chair as if it were on fire.

"Say no more, my life. I will get you two," he said. "You want a Sprite? I know they keep them back there."

"Do you think before you go to the nurse's station, you could sneak to a vending machine and get me a Coke? I doubt they would approve, but I could really use one."

"There are vending machines in the family waiting room," he said with a smile. "I will hit those up before I obtain your popsicles."

"Thank you," I said.

"I will return with your sugar buffet momentarily," Thorn said before he leaned down and kissed me, and then Laney, on our foreheads.

One of Meri's eyes opened. "Don't even think about it," he said.

"I wasn't," Thorn said with a chuckle.

He left the room, and I went back to flipping through the television channels. I eventually settled on the Weather Channel and watched as the storm system that had been terrorizing us moved off to the east.

"Thank goodness," I said. "I was wondering how long we'd be dealing with these storms."

"Something in the atmosphere has changed," Meri said.

"What do you mean?" I asked, but he'd slipped back into sleep.

Once they took the radar off the screen, I flipped past the Weather Channel. I must have gotten to the local news station because the name Coventry flipped across the screen.

I watched for a couple of minutes as they talked about the tornado and showed some of the devastation. Most of the footage included shots of the National Guard helping people. Next up was a story about local contractors all descending on Coventry to help with cleanup and rebuilding. There were dozens of companies all volunteering their time and what materials they could afford. The news lady said that several GoFundMe fundraisers had been set up to collect money for building materials as well.

"Looks like we're going to get a lot of help rebuilding," I said, but Meri was still snoozing away.

I was about to flip to another station when Stewart Randell's picture flashed on the screen. Instead of changing the station, I turned up the volume a little. Neither Meri nor Laney stirred.

The newscaster was dressed in a red blazer with red lipstick to match. Her hair was sprayed to within an inch of its life, and she talked about Stewart's death as if she were giving a traffic report.

She said that local law enforcement had interviewed the stepfather of the deceased's child. That was probably Jeremy, and she was talking about Dixon and his stepdad, John.

"Authorities release John Parker after the interview and will not confirm whether or not he's a person of interest in the case," the news anchor said as the station went to commercial.

Thorn came back into the room, and turned the TV volume back down. He set two Cokes down on my bed table and unwrapped a popsicle for me.

"Anything interesting?" He nodded toward the television and handed me the purple popsicle.

"Jeremy must have interviewed John Parker, but he wouldn't tell the news if he's a suspect or not," I said.

Thorn laughed. "You're in the hospital after just having our baby, and you're worried about a case."

"It just happened to be on the news," I said. "Swear."

"You should worry about other things," he said and patted my leg. "If I find a way to get you a cheeseburger, will you promise to stay out of this?"

"What do you know?" I asked and narrowed my eyes at him.

"Kinsley Wilson, what makes you think I know something?"

"One, you were gone too long to just buy a couple of Cokes and grab a popsicle from the nurse's station. Two, you're trying to bribe me with cheeseburgers. That means something. I know it," I said.

"Maybe the nurse just took a long time to get the popsicle. Hospital's filling up apparently. What if that's all it was?" he asked, but I could see he knew something.

"Spill it," I said as Laney opened her eyes and stretched. "Please," I whispered.

After a minute when Thorn was sure Laney wasn't going to wake up, he sighed and rubbed the bridge of his nose. "Fine, I do know that Jeremy interviewed John Parker, and I know that he's not in the clear. I actually remember him from right before the tornado. He was trying to cross the bridge I was guarding to get into

Coventry to pick up his stepson. I didn't know who he was at the time, but it all makes sense now."

"So, he was at the victim's house?" I asked.

"He was, and there's no way that he could have made it home before the storm hit. So, he was either at the victim's house, or he found somewhere to shelter in Coventry until it was over."

"The neighbors all acted clueless," I said.

"Doesn't mean they really were," Thorn said with a shrug.

"You think one of his neighbors was involved in the murder too?" I asked. "Or at least involved in helping cover it up?"

"Jeremy is handling the case," Thorn said and crossed his arms over his chest.

I was about to protest, but Laney beat me to it. She woke up, turned bright red, and let out a squawk that made Meri jump two feet in the air. Laney put her little fist in her mouth for a second but then pulled it out and began to wail.

"I think she's hungry," I said over the cacophony.

"Looks that way," Thorn said. "Let me get a bottle together really quick. You'll let me feed her this time?"

"Of course," I said.

I sang, or at least tried to sing, to Laney while Thorn got a bottle ready. When he had it done, I handed her over to him. She took the bottle right away, and I relaxed as he walked around the room feeding her and swaying softly. Thorn was a natural, and I could tell that Laney was going to be his little princess. It made my heart skip a beat to see them together.

When she finished her bottle, Thorn grabbed a cloth and sat down in the chair. He threw the cloth over his shoulder and burped her gently while I drank my Coke and fantasized about a cheeseburger.

"Is the cafeteria open at night here?" I whispered once she was asleep.

"I will get you a cheeseburger… and fries, but you have to promise to let the murder go," he said.

"Deal," I responded. "I really don't care about anything but our family. I swear."

"I know that," he said. "I just don't want you stressing yourself out over it. We'll be taking Laney home in a couple of days, and we need to rest and relax as much as we can while we're here. We won't have the nurses at home to help us."

"Oh, but we'll have my whole family," I said. "We'll have plenty of help, but I promise I won't stress over Stewart's death. Now, go get me a cheeseburger, manservant."

"Yes, ma'am."

Thorn stood up and handed Laney over to me. I must have drifted off a minute after he left, but I was awoken by a nurse gently taking Laney out of my arms.

"I'm just going to put her in the crib," she said and placed my baby in that clear plastic aquarium thing they called a crib. We both held our breath, but Laney didn't stir. "There now. You can get some rest. I saw your husband heading down the elevators a few minutes ago and figured I'd come check on you. Is he coming back tonight?"

"Yeah, he was just running down to the cafeteria to get... to get himself something to eat," I said and hoped she couldn't see I was fibbing.

"If you've farted, you can eat," she said and smiled at me.

It made me bust out laughing, but then I quickly covered my mouth. Fortunately, Laney was sleeping like a baby, and I didn't wake her.

"Sorry," the nurse said. "Someone should have told you that once you pass gas, you can eat. Means the surgeon didn't rearrange things in your gut, and it's safe."

"Right," I said. "Thank you."

"Not a problem. Let me know if you need anything."

She patted me on the shoulder, adjusted my blankets, and the left the room.

Thorn returned a short while later with two bags from the cafeteria. One had burgers and the other had some fresh, hot fries.

"I think I got it past them," he said as he plunked the bags down on my bed table.

"They said I could eat," I told him, but I left the other part out. Marriage required a bit of mystery. At least, I thought it did.

We ate our food, and I felt sleep pulling at me. Thorn told me to get some rest. "I can handle Laney if she wakes up. You need to heal."

It didn't take much prodding on his part. With my belly full of heavy food and a squirt from the morphine pump, I was out.

When I woke up, Thorn was rocking Laney by the window. The sun was well on the way to being up, and it sounded like he was softly whispering a story.

"You let me sleep all night?" I asked as I stretched and adjusted the bed to upright. "You didn't have to do that."

"I don't mind," he said and kissed Laney's head. "Miss Laney and I did just fine."

"I'm feeling better," I said. "I feel stronger today. I think I might be coming down with a cold, though. I've got a bit of a tickle in the back of my throat. I can't remember the last time I was sick. Maybe never."

"It's probably allergies. When it warms up like this, the allergens don't know it's not really spring. Or, it could be a mold allergy from all the rain. Now that you're not as magical, you might have to deal with them just like the rest of us."

"I'll ask the nurse for an allergy pill, then. What are you guys looking at?" I asked when I noticed that Thorn was still looking out the window.

"The warmer weather has a lot of people out. Lots of early morning walkers," he said as he turned back to me. "I should probably let you hold her for a while."

"That would be lovely," I said and stuck my arms out. "You can go home and shower if you want. I'm going to send Viv a text and see how Tangerine is doing. I've got to arrange them coming to visit too. Is the hospital really only allowing you and two others to visit? I can't sneak a couple more in?"

"I thought about it, but they're serious. The maternity ward is full, too. They had to call security yesterday when someone's feisty grandma refused to leave," Thorn said.

"Really? Okay, well, I don't want to be like that. I'll just have them come on rotation if they want. If they even all want to come here. Maybe they don't want to visit me in the hospital. Some people don't like it," I mused.

"Oh, no, they definitely do. Your mother and Lilith have already worked out a rotation. They will come back. Jeremy and Reggie are coming over together. Your dad and Viv are paired up. Dorian and Isaac are chomping at the bit to get here. It's all worked out, Kinsley. They are just waiting for you to give the go ahead and for visiting hours to start."

"Wow, so that sounds like a lot," I said, feeling suddenly overwhelmed.

"We can tell them no," Thorn said. "I will tell them no for you."

"No, that's okay, but I don't think I can handle more than that today. And maybe let them know short visits are better for now? We can all spend time together when I'm home."

"You're the boss," he said.

"You could go home and take a shower if you want," I offered.

"Do I smell?"

"No," I said with a chuckle. "But I didn't expect you to stay here for three days without leaving. I got to take a shower, but I don't think they'll let you use the one in here."

"You sure you don't mind? I'll stay right here with you the whole time," Thorn said.

"No, it's okay, but could you go down to the cafeteria first? Please get Meri some bacon," and at that, Meri's ears perked up.

"I can get something for you too," Thorn said.

"Another Coke, please. I can probably just eat whatever breakfast they bring me," I said.

"I'll see what they have down there," Thorn replied.

"Hey, Thorn," I said as I thought of something.

"What is it, babe?"

"What about the other Aunties? You didn't mention Amelda. I thought she'd want to come visit," I said.

"They're all throwing you a huge, over-the-top baby shower and welcome home party when you get out of here. Amelda was going to come up and visit with Remy, but she does have a cold. She figured it was better to just wait," Thorn said. "No sick people around Laney until she's had her vaccines."

"But what about me?" I asked.

"You've just got allergies," Thorn said. "But I'm going to head down to the cafeteria and get the cat bacon. I'll be back in a few."

"Thank you."

A couple of minutes after Thorn left, a nurse came in to check on us. She helped me change Laney's diaper and get a bottle ready.

"I think it's time for you to come off the pump," she said. "We'll switch you over to oral pain management now. Doctor's orders."

"I guess it couldn't last forever," I said.

"The upside is that it will be easier for you get up and move around. You can't really go anywhere, but at least you'll have your sea legs for when we do discharge you."

"You always hear those horror stories about women being discharged from the hospital hours after giving birth. Am I really going to be here for another two days?"

"The doctor might spring you tomorrow if things are looking good, but you're here at least tonight. I hate sending women home too early, but the ones that get sent home hours after didn't have a surgical birth. You get the deluxe treatment," she said.

"Thorn's got excellent insurance through his job too," I said.

"That definitely helps," she said. "Can I get you anything else."

"I've got a bit of a tickle in my throat. Can I get an allergy pill maybe?"

"Let me grab your vitals," she said. "I'm going to go get my thermometer."

She left and returned a minute later. Her thermometer was one she pressed against my forehead, but she did it three times. I could have sworn she'd gone a little pale but looked totally relieved after taking the reading.

"Right as rain," she said. "I'll get you an allergy pill added to your orders."

"What was wrong?" I asked. "You looked spooked. Should I be worried?"

"Not a bit, dear. We always have to watch for any signs of post-op infections. You've got no fever, so it's all good."

"You thought cold symptoms might be a post-op infection?" I was confused.

"Sometimes what new mothers think is just the sniffles is actually the beginning of pneumonia. I'm always super cautious. It's because of the anesthesia," she said.

"Oh, okay," I said.

"But you're fine. All that rain and mold spores really do get to people."

After that, she breezed out of the room and returned about twenty minutes later with an allergy pill and a small can of grape soda. I took the pill and then gave Laney the bottle the nurse had helped me prepare.

She was just about done with it when Thorn got back from the cafeteria. "The breakfast casserole they had on special looked amazing, so I got you some," he said. "Bacon for the cat in a little to-go container he can eat from."

"You're the best," I said. "Maybe you should take Meri with you when you go home to shower. It can't be good for him to be cooped up in this room."

"Not a chance," Meri groused. "I'm fine here."

"You're projecting," Thorn said with a chuckle. "You're sending me away and trying to send the cat away because you want to get out of here. Right?"

"Maybe," I said and realized he was probably right. "The nurse who was just here said that I might get to go home tomorrow. She turned off my morphine pump too."

"Bummer," Thorn said. "But wouldn't it be nice to go home tomorrow?"

"It would be. How long do you think you'll be gone?" I asked.

"Kinsley, I don't have to go," Thorn said.

"No, it's okay, really. I was just curious."

"I'll make it quick," Thorn replied.

Thorn was only gone for a little over an hour, but as soon as he got back, he got a call he had to step out into the hall to take.

"I have to go downstairs," Thorn said.

He'd just popped his head back in the door instead of coming all the way into the room.

"To the cafeteria?" I asked.

"To the morgue," he replied gravely.

"What?" I couldn't believe what I'd heard. "Is everything okay?"

"The medical examiner just finished his autopsy of Stewart Randell. He said he needs to go over his results, and he's about to rule on cause of death. I'm already in the hospital, so I thought it would be okay if I met with him. Is that all right? I can tell him no and get Jeremy over here," Thorn said.

"No, go, please. But you have to fill me in on what you find out," I said.

"We'll see," Thorn said and began to shut the door.

"Don't make me come down there," I said, but it was an idle threat. I wouldn't leave Laney even if the curiosity was about to kill me.

Thorn

I hated leaving Kinsley and Laney to work, but the medical examiner said that he had something important to tell me. He'd said it couldn't wait, so I rode the hospital elevator down to the basement and waited for the morgue attendant to buzz me in.

The hallway was overly bright and smelled of chemicals and cleaners. It was the first time I realized how tired I was, and I rubbed my eyes hoping to wake myself up.

Laney had slept most of the night, but she had woken up a couple of times. It wasn't just the sleep deprivation that was getting to me, though. I'd missed my morning run, and that exercise gave me energy. I needed the boost like I needed oxygen.

Something else was amiss too. There was a weird energy in the hospital, and it had my anxiety on alert. I hoped the doctor would send Kinsley home the next day because I wanted to get her and Laney away from whatever unspecified negative energy I'd felt.

I told myself it was just because it was a hospital. There'd been a lot of sickness and death there. Parts of the building were new and modern, like the morgue, but there were old parts too. Even the new morgue was just the old one remodeled. The energy under the surface was a hundred years old. Whatever old ghosts were there were probably just more confused by it all.

A shiver ran down my spine, but I didn't have time to dwell on it. The medical examiner stepped out into the hall from the autopsy area and greeted me.

"You're in the hospital because your wife gave birth?" he asked after we'd said our hellos and shook hands.

"Yes, a baby girl," I responded. "Mother and child are healthy and doing amazing."

"Congratulations," the ME said. "When does she get discharged?"

"Hopefully tomorrow," I said.

"That will be good," he said and cleared his throat. "I'm sure she'd love to get out of that room."

"I think so too," I said. "So, what brings me down here?"

He seemed to be lost in thought for a moment, but I'd met with that particular ME before. He could be a bit flaky.

"Right!" He said and he seemed to focus. "So, Stewart Randell wasn't murdered."

"What?" I nearly couldn't believe what I was hearing.

"You know that John Parker went to your station yesterday and confessed to your deputy that he'd thought about killing the deceased, but he said he ultimately backed out. They rode out the storm at the diner, and then went home," the ME said.

"That sounds like quite the story if I've ever heard one," I responded. "But no, Jeremy didn't tell me. Probably because of my wife having a baby."

"I thought that might be the case. Anyway, given the circumstances, I wanted to get the autopsy done as soon as possible. My findings back up what Mr. Parker said. No one murdered the deceased."

"What? How?" I asked. "He had a knife in his back."

"He also had a contusion and a laceration on his temple that were consistent with the edge of his countertop. Your deputy confirmed there was blood there."

"So, the killer bashed his head on the counter too," I said and pinched the bridge of my nose.

"Your deputy, Jeremy, also found that someone, probably the deceased, had loaded his knives into the dishwasher with the blades up. Was the dishwasher open when you found the body?" The ME asked.

"It was," I admitted. "I didn't really think about it at the time because it didn't seem relevant."

"Well, it was. Based on my examination, I'm ruling the death accidental. He appears to have tripped, hit his head, and fallen on one of the knives that he loaded blade up in the dishwasher. If I had to guess, based on pictures of the scene, I'd say he rolled off the dishwasher door and tried to crawl to his phone."

"But he was mostly paralyzed and bled out?" I asked.

"Exactly, and the contusion on his head didn't help. I found some pretty significant swelling on the brain. He must have been confused. In fact, if he hadn't bled out, I imagine the concussion would have killed him anyway," The ME concluded. "That's my official cause of death, and I'll be writing up the report ASAP."

With the official cause of death being listed as accidental, there was nothing more for my department to investigate. I called Jeremy and gave him the head's up before getting on the elevator and going back up to my wife and baby.

Epilogue

Kinsley

Thorn returned a half an hour after leaving to go to the morgue. With him, he brought a huge bouquet of pink roses and a fuzzy pink bear from the gift shop.

"Her first teddy bear," I said and nearly wept as he set the roses down on the table and handed me the bear. "I'll save it for when she's less likely to puke on it."

"Probably a good idea," Thorn said. "And, I've got even more good news."

"What's that?" I asked.

"I stopped by the cafeteria and perused the lunch specials. They're going to have beef lo mein and eggrolls," he said. "If you don't like that, they're also doing a Reuben and fries or your favorite, bacon cheddar burger and tater tots."

"Oooh, I think I'll do the lo mein, egg rolls, and a side of tater tots," I said. "Do they have milkshakes?"

"They do indeed," he said with a smile.

"I would kill for some ice cream," I said with a chuckle.

"No need to go that far, my love. As soon as they start serving lunch, I will bring you everything your heart desires," Thorn said.

"And while I appreciate that, you're still going to tell me what you found out from the medical examiner, right?" I asked with one eyebrow cocked.

"Of course," Thorn said with an overly dramatic sigh. "It's an interesting story."

He told me everything the ME had explained to him, and I nearly couldn't believe it. A familiar curiosity crept up on me, but then Laney stretched and let out a gurgle.

I let it go.

I had everything I needed right there in my arms. Well, also at my feet and next to my bed in an uncomfortable hospital chair.

"The roses are beautiful," I said. "Thank you so much."

"You're going to let this go?" Thorn asked skeptically.

"Of course, sweetie. There's nothing to hold onto. The case is closed and his death was tragic, but accidental. Dixon has a chance at a normal life now too. I hope he's able get past his father's death, but I think his life will be a lot easier now," I said. "He's got a loving family and a protective stepfather who won't let him ever come to any harm, right? I've got my family now too, and that's what matters to me."

"Is that going to be enough for you?" Thorn asked.

"How could it not be?" I asked. "For the rest of my life, Laney will always be my first priority. I'll leave the crime solving to you."

Thorn laughed. "We'll see," he said. "We'll just see."

I was going to say something snarky about him giving me a little credit, but Laney started to cry. It was time for a bottle and a diaper change. While Thorn was making her bottle, I changed her on the bed.

I couldn't believe how amazing it felt to be a mother. My heart was so full, I thought it would burst with happiness.

Meri walked up and licked Laney's forehead. Her little fist shot out and she snagged a tiny handful of his fir.

He took it well, and I smiled.

"A new little creature," he said, and I could swear I heard him begin to purr.

Thank you for reading!

Grab the first book in my snarky and suspenseful new series:

A Witch Named Hazel

Made in the USA
Coppell, TX
02 March 2021

51157324R00105